STELLA

STELLA

Hope Moskal

ISBN 978-1-105-63165-8

For Carol

The Snowman and the Telescope

It was a cold winter's day in Mayazure, but Stella Tyrian didn't feel the freezing temperature. The Welcome Garden was always as beautiful as a spring day. It wasn't until she stepped into the forest did she know the true weather. She had been coming to this great world for almost four months now, and she never missed a day. She enjoyed the second harvest festival and loved the crisp autumn months. Stella even helped celebrate Jerot Catosan's fortieth birthday with her grandmother, the Queen of Cobalian, and Tuptup, the head counselor to the Queen. Every night she would fall asleep only to wake up in Mayazure with Jerot waiting to greet her. Every morning he would wait for her in the Welcome Garden, and today was no exception. He was standing by the entrance wearing a wool cloak and hat to stay off the winter chill and in his hand was a long, black cloak for Stella.

"It's mighty cold today," Jerot said with a smile. "I thought you might need something extra."

Stella was only wearing jeans and the navy sweater that her grandmother knitted her. Just looking at Jerot in his winter clothes made her shiver. He wrapped the cloak around her before taking her hands in his.

"Thank you," Stella said, "I was a little chilly."

"I couldn't find any mittens," Jerot frowned as he looked at Stella's hands.

"It's okay. We won't be out here long."

All the trees were bare, and a thick coating of snow crunched beneath their feet as they walked out into the forest. Jerot helped Stella mount his

Friesian, and he mounted behind her as usual. He wrapped his cloak around Stella for extra protection before commanding his horse to walk down the brick path.

"What are you going to do this fine Sunday morning?" Jerot asked. Stella usually stayed in the castle with her grandmother in the morning while Jerot did his training exercises with the other knights.

"Well, we finished that puzzle yesterday," Stella said. "Maybe I can convince her to come out and make a snowman with me and the children." Stella loved the children of Cobalian. She taught them simple sculpting with clay and would play games with them when they weren't in school.

"Wish I could join you."

Stella giggled, "We can make another snowman together later."

"That's not what I meant," Jerot said as they took the left fork in the road. "I just want to spend all day with you instead of just the afternoon."

"Oh," Stella felt awkward. Memories of their kiss crept into her mind. She tried very hard to forget it, but her feelings for Jerot weren't changing. She was still very much in love with him. "It could be worse, you could not see me at all."

"My life would be over if that ever happened," Jerot whispered.

His words left an uncomfortable silence that lasted until they reached the wall of Cobalian. The white wall was so brilliant that it made the surrounding snow look gray in comparison. Stella placed her right hand on the blue marble heart in the center of the golden gate. Her grandmother's ring shimmered, and the gate opened.

Cobalian was a winter wonderland; garlands of evergreen draped everything with branches of holly and mistletoe scattered about. Christmas would soon be here, and the civilians were getting into the spirit. Jerot steered his horse to the stables where Dekel, Jerot's apprentice, was waiting.

"Good morning, Dekel," Stella said as she slid off the horse.

"Morning, ma'am," Dekel said. Jerot handed the reins to him, and he walked the horse to its stall. Jerot escorted Stella through the trade quarter. People walked about, shopping at vendors for daily supplies or Christmas presents. Stella spotted a few kids running in the snow, throwing snowballs and trying to shove each other under a sprig of mistletoe. When they reached the topaz walkway to the castle, Jerot turned to her. He placed his hands on her upper arms and gently rubbed them for warmth.

"I guess this is goodbye," he said.

"For now."

Jerot smiled. He leaned forward and kissed Stella on the forehead; the butterflies in her stomach fluttered briefly with excitement. "I'll see you at lunch then," he said before letting her go.

Stella walked up the topaz walkway to the main door of the castle. She greeted the two guards who opened the door and then looked back to give one final wave, but Jerot was already gone, blended into the crowd of people living their daily lives. Stella felt an ache of sadness.

Stella's grandmother and Tuptup were enjoying a breakfast of French toast when she entered the throne room. A large Christmas tree, decorated with blue and silver, had been erected by the balcony. Tuptup greeted her and removed her cloak.

"Good morning," he said, "come sit down and get warm."

"Have a pleasant trip?" Queen Iona asked.

Stella thought back on her depressing conversation with Jerot. "More cold than pleasant, I suppose," she said.

"Oh? Is something wrong?"

"No, no," Stella sat down at the mahogany table next to her grandmother, "it just was uncomfortable, because Jerot couldn't find any mittens for me."

"Well, we can fix those cold hands," Tuptup said, pouring Stella a cup of tea.

Stella gorged herself on French toast and sausage. Tuptup was the best cook, and Stella just couldn't help herself from overeating. She listened to her grandmother and Tuptup discuss plans for Christmas in Cobalian. Some of the local women completed a Santa suit, but no one had yet volunteered for the job. A group of knights managed to find some reindeer in a goblin city to the west and borrowed them for the occasion.

"Do they fly?" asked Stella.

"Huh?" Tuptup seemed confused, "Of course they fly. Never heard of a reindeer that couldn't."

"They don't on Earth, unfortunately," said Queen Iona.

"Really?" Tuptup said. "That is a shame."

After everyone was full, Stella was able to convince the other two to go outside and make a snowman with the children.

"Oh what fun," said Queen Iona. "I haven't made a snowman in years."

Once bundled up in wool cloaks and hats and mittens, they headed into the town square. The snow was perfect for building a snowman. Stella started a small ball of snow and began to roll it across the ground while Tuptup started another. Soon, children began to join in, helping to push the large snowballs. Once Stella felt hers was big enough, she started a third, while Tuptup placed his snowball on top of the first. One passersby donated coal and twigs, and a vegetable vendor gave the Queen a carrot for the nose. Once the three snowballs were in place, the Queen used the coal and the carrot to complete a face and the twigs for the arms. The snowman was seven feet tall, the largest Stella had ever built.

"He looks chilly," said Queen Iona. Tuptup removed his cloak for Stella to put on the snowman, and Stella sacrificed her hat to cover his smooth, white head.

"There, much better," Stella stood back to admire the creation. A snowball hit her square in the back. "Hey!" Stella turned around to see her grandmother laughing. *So, she wants to play rough?* Stella thought. She reached down and grabbed some snow. She aimed for the old woman but decided at the last minute to throw the snowball at Tuptup, hitting him square in the face and making him fly backwards onto the ground. Laughter erupted at Tuptup's embarrassment. He made his own snowball and threw it at one of the children.

In that instant, a free-for-all snowball fight ensued. White balls of coldness sailed every which way. Tuptup grabbed snow and literally flung it; there was no time for neatness. Stella packed a snowball and turned, ready to throw it at who was behind her—it was Jerot.

"Oh," Stella was surprised, "is it noon already?"

"Pretty much," Jerot smiled. "Nice snowman." Before Stella could thank him, a snowball hit Jerot in the back of the head. He turned in anger, "Who threw that?"

The group of children scattered like cockroaches, except one little girl. She stood frozen in fear, as if she too was made of snow.

"I'm sorry," her voice shook. "I meant to hit Stella."

The anger drained from Jerot's face. He knelt down and wiped a tear from the little girl's cheek. "It's okay," he said, "but next time you do that, I might have to get the Tickle Monster to come and eat you!" Jerot tickled the little girl and she giggled before running off to join the other children.

Tuptup prepared chili for lunch with homemade bread and fresh butter. Stella let the steam warm her face before digging in. She was impressed by the way Jerot had treated the little girl. He had no children, but he seemed to know how to deal with them. Once everyone was full of chili, conversation arose.

"What are your plans this afternoon?" Queen Iona asked Stella and Jerot.

"I don't know," Stella was too relaxed to think or do anything. "It's too cold to fish and we weren't going to see Mullitor until Friday."

"We should work on your archery," Jerot said, still chewing bread. Stella cringed at the thought. She loved archery and was getting quite good, but she found Jerot's constant hovering to be very annoying. However, her interest in the sport has brought Jerot to take it up again himself. He had entered the archery tournament during the second harvest festival and won third place, which wasn't bad for someone who hadn't used his bow in years.

"I guess, if you think the weather is okay," Stella said.

"Well, if you get too cold, you can always come inside for tea," Queen Iona said, "I have some reading to catch up on."

Stella and Jerot headed down through the castle and made their way to the armory tent, a large tent filled with hundreds of different weapons. If a knight couldn't afford to buy a weapon, he was free to borrow one from the armory tent. Stella walked past the racks of bows and found her favorite: a self bow made of elm. She grabbed a quiver of arrows and joined Jerot outside.

The targets were lined up next to the tent, as were the training dummies that the knights use to test swords. Jerot had already measured out twenty paces from the targets and drawn a line in the snow with his foot.

"That's a good starting distance," he said. "Now, let's work on that form." Stella took an arrow and set it in her bow. She raised the bow and took aim at the target. Jerot stood beside her, their cheeks barely touching as he checked her aim. "I notice you are always shooting right of center," he gently moved her bow arm a little to the left. "Let's try that and see what we get. Don't be afraid to pull the arrow back as far as you can. You won't break the string," Jerot lifted Stella's string elbow. "Don't slouch your elbow or you'll shoot over the target."

"Okay, okay," Stella's voice revealed a hint of aggravation. Jerot stood back and crossed his arms. She pulled back the arrow and, after a pause of concentration, let it go. The arrow flew straight at the target, hitting the ring just below the bull's eye. "Hitting low is better than to the right, correct?"

"Why do you do that?" Jerot asked as he walked over to pull out the arrow.

"Do what?" Stella asked, feeling frustrated. She had done everything right.

"You hold your breath when you shoot. I've noticed that you have been doing that lately," Jerot wiggled the arrow in his hand, accentuating his words. "When you hold your breath, you cut off oxygen to the brain, which makes your eyes lose focus and your muscles weaken. If you breathe correctly, I bet you would hit better." Stella rolled her eyes. She felt like she was back in high school, being lectured for every mistake.

"Fine, Mr. Know-it-all," Stella pouted. "Can you please show me the proper way?"

"Gladly," Jerot took her bow and set a new arrow.

"You're slouching your elbow," Stella muttered as Jerot took aim. He shot her a 'don't be a smartass' look.

"It's quite simple. You inhale as you pull back the arrow," Jerot said, "and exhale as you release." He let the arrow go and it hit the top of the bull's eye.

"Told you, you're slouching your elbow," Stella seemed pleased with herself. Jerot handed her the bow back.

"Work on your breathing."

Stella began to practice while Jerot stood back, watching in silence. She liked it better when Jerot wasn't always interrupting her. Jerot's words echoed in her head, *inhale as you pull back the arrow and exhale as you release.* Unfortunately, she would forget something else while concentrating on her breathing, and the arrow would either go too far to the right or too high. After an hour, Jerot had decided Stella had had enough frustration.

"I'm cold, let's go in the tent and warm up a bit," he said.

"Did I improve at all?" Stella struggled, pulling out the last arrow from the target. Jerot assisted her in prying it out.

"Improvement takes time. Once you master the technique, accuracy will follow."

Stella placed her bow back on the rack while Jerot took out a sword made of wood. It was something the children could play with, but Jerot felt like lightening the mood a bit. He waved the sword out in front of him and closed his left eye as if wearing an eye patch.

"Argh! I be Captain Catosan, ruler of the sixteen seas. Hand over ye ship or prepare to be splintered to death."

"Oh, is that so?" Stella laughed. She lifted another wooden sword.

"I beg your pardon," she said in a British accent. "You cannot have this ship for it belongs to the King of England."

"Where?"

"It's a country on Earth," Stella explained, "now, *en garde!*"

They playfully fenced and even though Jerot was an exceptional swordsman, he went easy on Stella. Jerot would throw in an occasional 'Argh!' that made Stella laugh. Finally, she was able to poke him in the chest with the tip of her sword. Jerot dropped to his knees.

"Oh, you got me," he laid down on the ground. Stella kneeled down beside him, "My child," Jerot grabbed Stella by the front of her sweater, "avenge my death and kill the King of…" Jerot broke out of character, "what was it called?"

"England."

"Oh, yeah right," he continued, "kill the King of England." Jerot collapsed in feign death; his eyes closed and his tongue hung out. Stella giggled.

"You're a horrible actor," she said. Jerot opened his eyes and smiled.

The rest of the afternoon they fenced with the wooden swords. Jerot showed Stella different moves and how to parry. He seemed more relaxed than when teaching her archery. Perhaps it was because Jerot expected archery to be her calling, her profession. Sword fighting was merely play.

"Want to go for a walk?" Jerot asked, after a while.

"Yes. All this fighting has made me hot," Stella put the swords away. "Where to?"

Jerot shrugged, "Just around the city. Maybe we can find a place to build our own snowman, if you still want to." Stella smiled.

They left the armory tent and walked their way through the trade quarter. Every so often, a vendor's tent would catch Stella's eye and she would have a look at what they were selling. Everyone knew that the Queen would reimburse the vendors for whatever Stella would take, but mostly it was just food. Stella wasn't sure anything she bought would come home with her. Many times, Jerot offered to buy a gift for her, but she never let him; it could be taken the wrong way.

At the southern edge of the quarter, a group of people were sitting on logs around a small bonfire. One of the women–a petite lady with shoulder-length gray hair–spotted Jerot and Stella and called out to them.

"Jerot," said the woman, "would you both like to join us for some hot chocolate?"

"Oh, I could use something to drink," said Stella. They walked over to the group, who shifted to make room on one of the logs.

"I haven't seen you in a few weeks, Sandra," Jerot said to the woman. "Thought maybe you were hibernating for the winter this year." Sandra chuckled as she lifted the kettle warming by the fire and made each of them a cup of hot chocolate.

Stella drank and listened as people talked about their Christmas plans and about the Santa dilemma.

"I think Bernard the blacksmith should play Santa," suggested a blond-haired woman. "He's a big guy. He'd be perfect."

"Yes, he does meet the physical requirements, Julie," said Sandra, "but he lacks experience with children. He might be too rough."

"Maybe you can do it, Jerot," said Stella, remembering his encounter with the little girl earlier.

"Oh, no!" Jerot shot down the idea immediately. "I am a person of high authority. The last thing I need is to humiliate myself in a red suit."

"But no one would know it was you."

Jerot firmly shook his head, causing laughter amongst the group. The conversation turned to a new subject. Charles, an elderly man sitting next to Stella, talked about the upcoming wedding of his daughter and all the plans that still needed to be made. Stella started to daydream about the planning of her own wedding.

"Tell me, Jerot," Julie interrupted, "When are you going to marry this wonderful girl here?"

The blunt and unexpected question made Jerot choke on his hot chocolate. Stella quickly patted him on the back. She could feel her cheeks burning and it wasn't because of the fire or the hot chocolate. Several of the women giggled at Jerot's reaction.

"We're just friends," said Stella while Jerot continued to cough, "Besides, I'm already married."

"Oh," Julie blushed and some of the ladies looked disappointed, "It's just that…" she hesitated, "You look so cute together."

Stella knew what Julie really wanted to say: That she looked like Saura, Jerot's late wife. It was no secret; Stella had been hearing the whispers for months about her similarities to Saura. She tried to ignore them. She knew who she was, but it was hard to convince everyone else, including Jerot.

"Cute?" Jerot finally managed to speak. "I think all the cuteness is one-sided," he winked at Stella. *Oh, you're not helping the situation*, she thought.

"Oh, don't be silly," said Sandra. "You are still a very handsome man. I bet women are lined up to date you." Before Jerot could respond, the clock tower chimed five o'clock.

"We should go," Stella took this as a prime opportunity. "I'm sure the Queen is expecting us for dinner." Jerot followed her lead.

"Yes, she gets quite grumpy if we're late." They said goodbye to the group and left quickly.

Dinner was exquisite as always, but Jerot wasn't eating. He poked at the pork chop with his fork. Stella was busy talking to her grandmother, but Tuptup noticed.

"You can stab it all you want," he said. "But it's as dead as it's going to get."

"Is something wrong, dear?" asked Queen Iona. "Is the pork chop too dry?" Tuptup gave an offended snort.

"No," Jerot pushed his plate away. "I guess I'm not that hungry."

"Not hungry?" the Queen rose up out of her chair and went over to feel

Jerot's forehead, much to his dismay. "Well, you don't have a fever."

"I'm fine. Really." Jerot drank wine from his goblet.

Stella knew he wasn't fine. Was he thinking about what Julie had said? Were her words haunting him? Stella suddenly lost her appetite as well, and pushed her plate away.

"I guess we shouldn't have had that hot chocolate, huh?" Stella said. "I'm getting full myself."

After dinner, the Queen asked Tuptup and Jerot to gather the books that were piled up around her throne and take them downstairs to the library.

"Did you read all of these today?" Jerot asked, as Tuptup stacked them up in his arms.

"No," Queen Iona giggled. "But I did need them all for reference."

"What are you looking for?" Stella asked her.

"A piece of Cobalian history. Something I was curious about."

"Oh," Stella didn't care for history.

After Tuptup and Jerot left, Stella and her grandmother worked on their knitting. Stella was horrible at it; her fingers were just not flexible enough to work the needles and her nervousness would cause her hands to sweat. After several minutes of struggle, she set the needles down and watched her grandmother knit a hat of pale blue.

"What's wrong with Jerot?" Queen Iona words broke the silence of the room.

"Huh? Oh…" Stella had already forgotten his strange behavior at dinner. "One of the women we ran into said something about how we look cute together as a couple. I think he took that to heart."

"He hasn't quite accepted the fact that you are not Saura, has he?" Queen Iona's needles clicked away.

"No," Stella watched the bulbs on the Christmas tree reflect the light from the setting sun, "and it's small things like that that will prevent him from doing so."

"And have you been on your best behavior?"

"Grandma!" Stella was shocked, "Of course I have. I'm not like that." It was true. Stella always refused Jerot's advancements. Almost every day he would ask for a kiss, but Stella stood firm on her loyalty to her husband Ryan, even if it was tempting.

"He just needs more time," said Queen Iona. "Even ten years of mourning is not enough."

By the time Tuptup and Jerot returned, the sun had set and the stars were beginning to play in the sky. Tuptup was holding a few new books. He set them down on the mahogany table while Jerot walked out to the balcony.

"Here are some more for you," Tuptup said.

"Thank you, dear," said Queen Iona. She watched Jerot looking at the stars, a slight frown on her face. Stella watched Jerot with sadness. "You know," Queen Iona called over to Jerot, "I've just had the telescope fixed on the Astronomy Tower, if you would like a closer look." Jerot turned and smiled.

"Stella, I could show you some of the constellations," Jerot said.

"Oh, well, that does sound like fun," she said. Anything was better than knitting. Jerot took her hand and they walked through the silver door.

"Don't stay out too late now," Queen Iona said with a chuckle.

Stella wasn't sure what her grandmother's intentions were. She always warned Stella not to get attached to Jerot, and yet never stopped them from being alone together. The constant emotional tug-of-war confused Stella on what was the right thing to do.

Jerot led Stella down the hall and into the foyer. They moved down two doors to the right and entered a short hallway almost twenty feet long, which ended in another spiral staircase. Up and up they went, until the staircase ended at a trap door. Jerot pushed open the door and stepped up to the observation deck of the tower, before helping Stella up. The rooftop was

open to the sky, edged by a four-foot
wall. A massive telescope was
mounted on a tripod in the center.
The black sky stretched out above
them, studded with stars. It was more
impressive than any planetarium.

Stella looked to her left and saw
the throne room tower; the balcony
was on the other side, which meant
neither her grandmother nor Tuptup
could see them. She looked over the
wall and could see the entire castle.
Several towers stabbed into the sky,
but none were as tall as the one they
were standing on.

"Come here," said Jerot. He was
adjusting the telescope and had found
something he wanted to share. "This
is a great view of the planet Idzic."

Stella removed her glasses and
peered into the eyepiece of the
telescope. Once in focus, she was able
to see a planet of swirling green fog.
For an hour, Jerot showed Stella
different constellations and planets.
Stella was enjoying the bright purple
planet called Vicerian, when Jerot
changed the mood.

"Stella," the way he said her name. She had heard it so many times before. It was the tone he used whenever he wanted a kiss, or to tell her how much he loved her. She looked away from the telescope. Without her glasses, he was fuzzy in shape, as if an angelic aura surrounded him.

"Please don't," Stella whispered. Her mouth was dry from the awkwardness of the situation. They were completely alone and the trap door was behind Jerot. There was really no escape.

"I can't help it," Jerot came closer and Stella was able to see him more clearly, "What Julie said earlier is still in my head. She's right. We should be together."

"Only because I look like…" Stella didn't want to say Saura's name in front of Jerot. It always upset him more, so it became almost a forbidden word, "…like her. I'm not a replacement. I'm my own person."

"I know that," Jerot's words shocked Stella, "The more I'm with you, the more I am falling for you. I will always love Saura," his voice cracked slightly from saying the name, "but I'm beginning to see the true person in front of me and I want you to know that I have feelings for you. I think you might feel the same way about me."

Stella closed her eyes for a moment. Jerot's suspicions were true: She was falling more and more in love with him every day. She opened her eyes and put her glasses back on. Though the stars were the only light, Stella could see Jerot's pleading blue eyes.

"You are a wonderful friend," Stella said, "But I don't feel that way for you." Her words ate at her; she hated to lie. "I am with Ryan, I can't be with you." Jerot took her hands in his. Stella could feel his hands were shaking.

"Are you sure?" Tears filled his eyes. Stella felt guilt wash over her. "Can you at least think about it?"

"I have."

"I want nothing more than to kiss you again."

"No," Stella answered firmly. She hadn't kissed him since that night at his home, almost four months ago. "If I do that, it will only make things worse. You need to understand that we can't be together." Jerot lowered his head. Stella could feel his tears falling on their clasped hands.

"I will respect your decision," Jerot looked up to met Stella's eyes. His tears had left streaks on his face. Stella wiped them away with the sleeve of her sweater.

The clock rang the hour. Stella didn't pay enough attention to count the chimes, but she knew it was late. She shivered in the wind.

"We should go back," said Stella, "I have to go home. I have my last class for the semester tomorrow."

"I will see you tomorrow?" Jerot always asked this question at the end of the day.

"Of course," Stella smiled, "You still owe me a snowman."

They left the observation deck and descended the staircase before walking out into the foyer.

"I will take my leave here," Jerot said. "Tell everyone I said good night."

"I will," Stella hesitated slightly before kissing Jerot on the cheek. His warm skin against her lips made her heart jump in excitement. She wanted to kiss him more than he wanted to kiss her, but she felt this was an acceptable middle ground. They smiled at each other before Jerot left through the main door and Stella made her way to the throne room.

The Sketchbook

Stella awoke to the sound of her alarm clock. She smacked it and attempted to roll over, but something heavy weighed on her chest. She pulled the covers off her head to see it was Roxanne, the calico Persian she and Ryan pampered. She was sitting on Stella's chest, refusing to budge until she knew for sure she was going to get fed.

"I suppose you want me to wake up," Stella addressed the blurry image of Roxanne.

Once Roxanne knew she had Stella's attention, she jumped down off the bed so Stella could get up. Stella put on her glasses. She was now at home on Earth. Her husband, Ryan, was in the shower already, trying his best Luciano Pavarotti impersonation. Stella chuckled and followed Roxanne down the stairs to the kitchen.

Stella fed the cat and prepared breakfast as usual. She whipped up omelets and sausage to the sound of Roxanne slurping up her cat food. Stella poured orange juice and set the dining room table. Before breakfast was ready, Roxanne was gone, leaving nothing but an empty dish that looked just as clean as when Stella last washed it.

"Pig," Stella muttered, picking up the plate and placing it in the sink.

She could take her time in the morning, since her one class didn't start until ten o'clock. Today was the last class and Stella was more excited than ever. She was going to show the students an example for their final sculpture, but it wasn't just any example. It was her masterpiece, her 'baby,' her most precious treasure. She had spent more time on this sculpture than any other; her legacy would be contained in this one piece.

Ryan came down just as Stella was serving the omelets. He was wearing a suit, as he wore every day for his job at the Cleveland Insurance Company. He greeted Stella with a kiss and she straightened his tie out of habit.

"Made you an omelet just the way you like it," Stella said.

"You spoil me," Ryan nibbled at her ear.

"No, I spoil the cat. I take care of you."

They ate breakfast as snow fell outside. Stella watched it swirl around the backyard through the patio window. The view was nothing like the one through Jerot's dining room window, but it was still pretty.

"I have to call the travel agency," Ryan said. "Our plane tickets should be in soon." They had planned on a vacation to Las Vegas for a week before Christmas. Neither of them had taken a vacation since their honeymoon, though Stella felt she was on vacation every time she slept. It still would be nice to just get away from it all, even other worlds. She was planning on leaving the ring at home so she wouldn't lose it or worse, have it get stolen. Stella had yet to tell her grandmother of the trip, and she definitely didn't tell Jerot.

"And the hotel?" asked Stella.

"All set. They charged the deposit on my credit card."

"I can't wait to lie by the pool and get away from all this snow," Stella picked up the empty plates and glasses and set them in the sink. Ryan packed up his briefcase before kissing Stella goodbye.

"I'll call you later to see how class went." Ryan always called Stella at her office after class. She liked the way he always checked on her; he was so thoughtful.

"Okay," Stella said, "You do that."

After Ryan left, Stella did the dishes and went back upstairs to get dressed. She removed her grandmother's ring and placed it carefully in her silver jewelry box before heading to the shower. She rarely wore it during the day for fear of anything happening to it. It was her only gateway to her grandmother and if it were to be damaged or lost, Mayazure would be gone forever.

Roxanne watched as Stella dried her hair and braided it. Stella threw on a pair of jeans and a dressy green sweater. There was not going to be any dirty work today. She gave Roxanne a pat on the head.

"Be a good girl. I'll be back this afternoon," Stella said.

Downstairs, she wrapped up in a heavy wool coat and gloves, grabbed her purse and got into her little sports car. Traffic was horrendous, as always. Trying to drive anywhere near the university was always a challenge. If it wasn't the slow-moving cars, it was the students, jay-walking across the busy roads on their way to classes. The snow on the roads was not helping the situation; apparently, the snowplows had yet to clear the roads. Stella gripped the steering wheel, making her knuckles turn white, until she was safe in her parking spot behind the art building.

Stella walked through the back doors and glanced at the clock on the wall. She always looked at that clock as soon as she walked through those doors. She prided herself on never being late and today was no exception: she was ten minutes early.

Stella walked down the hall and up to the second floor before turning right towards the sculpture department. She passed the glass wall of the gallery, where some student pieces were displayed. Every month, the teachers would pick a student's artwork from each class to be placed in the gallery. It was an honor to be picked. Stella looked past her reflection in the glass and saw the small plaster sculpture that one of her students had made. It was an abstract swirl of multiple colors (the assignment was to show movement) on a small pedestal. The student's name, the name of the class and Stella's name were printed on a tiny place card next to the sculpture.

Stella stopped at her office to hang up her coat and purse. She locked the door and continued to the end of the hall, where her classroom was. She opened the door and flicked on the lights. Twenty large wooden desks were set up in neat rows with Stella's desk sitting in front of the chalkboard. The back of the room was lined with cabinets of supplies and a utility sink. Shelves were mounted on one wall, displaying several of Stella's sculptures. Many of them were used as models for weekly projects. Stella walked to the end of the top shelf and took down a box. This was her pride and joy: her greatest work. So secret, she kept it hidden in this box. So precious, it had to be protected from harm.

Stella carefully placed the box on her desk. She hummed the melody of the second movement to Dvorak's Ninth Symphony as she wrote the word *Emotion* in big letters on the chalkboard. This was to be the final assignment for her students: to capture an emotion in an inanimate object. Stella opened the top of the box and looked inside, smiling in satisfaction.

The students began to trickle in. Many of them were freshman who took the class only for an art credit, but they had enjoyed it. Soon, the desks were full. A group of girls were chatting while others were unpacking notebooks or looking at their planners. Since the class was going to be short, Stella decided to wait a few more minutes before starting, to build suspense.

"Okay everyone, listen up," Stella said finally. The students hushed and gave her their complete attention. "Today's class is going to be short and there will be no more classes this week." Some of the boys whispered "Yes!" and a few high-fived each other. "However," Stella continued, "I am giving you your final assignment, which is due in my office a week from today at 5 pm. I will grade them by January 2, and you will have until February 28 to pick up your sculptures. After that, they become part of my 'home collection'." Several students wrote down the dates in their notebooks. Stella continued.

"Your final project centers around emotion," Stella pointed to the chalkboard, "I want you to take a material void of life and give it a soul, feeling, emotion. You can use any material that we have studied this semester: ceramic, metal, plaster, etc. This will give you a chance to use what you know best. Your subject can be a person, an animal, even something that doesn't exist," Stella smiled, "just as long as I can feel what the subject is feeling. You can choose any emotion you like: happiness, sadness, anger. The choices are infinite. Now, let me show you an example."

Stella opened the box and reached inside. She carefully removed a clay sculpture that was set on a mahogany base. It was a dragon. The body was stained purple, so dark it was almost black. Emeralds were set into his eye sockets. A small gold plaque was located on the base that read *Mullitor*. Several of the students oh'd and ah'd.

One boy whispered, "Wow, that is wicked cool."

"Now, I know you are all beginners here," Stella said as she placed the sculpture on her desk, "So I don't expect you to create anything like this, but I wanted to show you how good you can become someday. The point is not to make the object perfect, but to make the emotion real." Stella leaned against her desk, "Can anyone tell me what emotion my dragon is feeling?" Hands rose up in the air. Stella pointed to the blonde girl in the front, "Yes, Molly."

"He's sad," Molly said.

"And how can you tell?"

Molly looked hard at the sculpture, "He's looking down at his hands."

The miniature version of Mullitor was holding up his front paws. His head was bent down looking at them forlornly. "Very good," Stella said, "Now, why is he looking at his hands?" A boy in the third row waved his hand eagerly, Stella called on him, "Go ahead, Jack."

"He looks like he's missing something," Jack said, "He's lost something very important and he's lamenting it."

"Excellent," Stella smiled. Her students seemed never to fail her. "Let me tell you this dragon's story," Stella gently placed her hand on the dragon's head. "Mullitor here has lost all his family and friends. They have all died and he is the last one of his kind. He longs to find their corpses so that they can have a proper burial and their souls can rest. He is sad, not only because he can't bury them, but also because he knows their souls are troubled."

"That really is sad," said the girl next to Molly.

Stella nodded, "That is also part of the final project. I want you to write a short back-story to help explain your sculpture and to point out key elements as to how it shows the emotion you chose." Several students groaned. "I know, I know," Stella said, "This is not a writing class. I'm not going to grade you on grammar here, and I don't want anything longer than one page. I hate to read just as much as you hate to write." The students laughed, "Are their any questions?" The girl next to Molly raised her hand, "Yes, Emma."

"Do we have to create a story ourselves?" asked Emma.

"I would prefer that you do," Stella said, "but, if you read a book by someone else and you want to sculpt something from a scene that you liked, don't be afraid to do so. Also, look at photos of animals and people expressing the emotion you want to sculpt. Study their facial characteristics and muscle structure. Looking in the mirror helps too. Any other questions?" No one else raised their hand, "Okay, if you do have questions, I will be keeping my office hours the same this week, so feel free to stop in."

Stella packed up her sculpture as the students gathered their belongings and filed out of the classroom. Once the tiny Mullitor was safely back on the top shelf, Stella left the room and walked back down to her office. She sat down at her desk and looked at the clock on the wall. Ryan would probably not call for another thirty minutes. Stella opened the drawer in her desk and pulled out a sketchbook and a pencil.

When Stella wasn't grading projects or counseling a student, she drew in her sketchbook. Drawing was her second favorite medium, next to sculpting. She could close her eyes and let the pencil take over, creating paths of graphite that took shape of whatever was in her head. Many of Stella's drawings became sculptures; they were the two-dimensional drafts.

Stella closed her eyes and took a deep breath. The image of a man with dark hair and piercing blue eyes formed in her mind: Jerot. She missed him most when she had nothing else to keep her mind occupied. She looked at the blank page before her and began to draw a few curved lines. A few moments later Stella closed her eyes again, deep in thought before drawing some more. She drew a sort of fancy stick figure, with legs slightly apart and one arm straight out to the side while the other was pulled back.

Stella again closed her eyes and leaned back in her chair. Her memory took her back to the second harvest festival. She remembered sitting in the stands at the tournament. The crowd waved red, yellow and brown flags: the colors of the season. Her memory of Jerot during the archery tournament flashed in her mind, his perfect form and near perfect accuracy. Stella checked her drawing to compare it with her mental image. After a slight adjustment, she began filling in the details.

Stella crouched over the page, scratching away with her pencil. She paused every so often to close her eyes and check her memory before sketching more. Eyes, nose, shoulders, chest, hands; the body parts began to take form. A half-complete Jerot was on the page before the ringing phone interrupted her.

"Hello?"

"Hi, it's just me," Ryan said on the other end. "How was class?"

"Class was fine," Stella closed her sketchbook, shutting Jerot out of her mind. "I gave the kids their final project. I will probably stay here until one o'clock, just in case anyone shows up with questions. Did you call the Travel Agency?"

"Yep, the tickets are here. I'll pick them on my lunch hour," Ryan's voice was full of excitement. "A week from tomorrow, we'll be on a plane."

Stella sighed, "I hate flying." This wasn't entirely true. She hated flying on a plane. She loved flying on Mullitor's back; looking down at all of Mayazure. Flying on a dragon was much more fun and less likely to crash.

"You'll do fine," Ryan said. "It's only a four hour plane ride. I'm sure they'll show a good movie to keep everyone's mind off the fact that they are thousands of feet up in the air."

Stella groaned, "Thanks for the pleasant thought."

"Sorry."

Once they said their goodbyes, Stella opened up her sketchbook again. She looked at the drawing of Jerot. What was he doing right now? Most likely sleeping. Was he having sweet dreams or violent nightmares? Did he toss and turn at night? Maybe he snores or talks in his sleep. What does he talk about? What does he wear to bed? Does he wear anything at all? Stella shook her head of that last thought and continued to draw.

After thirty minutes, Stella's pencil sketch was complete. Jerot stood before her, his bow held out with an arrow pulled back, ready to fire. She opened the drawer of her desk and pulled out colored pencils. She made his skin deep tan, and his eyes as bright blue as she could. She lightly streaked his black hair with gray and smudged it with her fingers to blend together. She colored his doublet a deep plum, and his pants black.

Stella gazed at her work. She gently caressed his face with her fingers. The paper was rough and cold, nothing like his real skin, so soft and warm. Her fingers ran down his shoulders and chest. His real muscles were strong, but here they were flat and powerless. The image was beautiful, but nothing compared to the real thing. Stella sighed and closed the sketchbook.

Again, Stella leaned back in her chair, boredom consuming her. She could feel her stomach complain; the omelets was so long ago. She reached into her purse, pulled out a dollar bill from her wallet, and left her office, walking back past the gallery and into the professors' lounge area. Stella wasn't much for eating from the vending machines, but when her stomach demanded food, she had no choice. A few of the other art professors were in the lounge sitting at a round table, eating lunches that they had brought from home. Stella greeted them warmly before walking to the glowing machines. None of the processed pre-packaged items you would call food interested her; it was either high carbohydrate starches or sugar infused candies. Stella decided on a bag of pretzels, probably the healthiest thing in there. She inserted the dollar into the machine and jabbed at the keypad below, punching in the code to make that metal spiral twist, releasing its chemically altered prisoner to the tray below.

With treat in hand and change in her pocket, Stella walked back towards her office. She munched on the hard salt-covered breadsticks as she walked past the gallery. As usual, the glass wall between her and the displays reflected her faint mirror image as she passed, but it was a second image, which flashed by in an instant, that made her stop. She swore she saw it: The glimpse of a thin woman with long blonde hair. Stella stood still, pretzel hanging from her mouth, staring into the glass. Was her hunger making her see things? Stella retraced her steps and walked along side the glass wall a second time, but all she saw this time was her own reflection looking back. She turned and looked around. Class was in session, so the hallway was completed deserted.

Whom did she see? Stella continued to her office, frowning. It was one thing to travel to another world while she slept every night, but to see things that weren't there? That was a sign of insanity.

Stella made it to her office and shut the door. She looked at the clock and noticed she still had forty-five minutes left before the end of her office hours. *I think I might have to shorten office hours today*, she thought, *I must not be feeling well.* Stella packed up her things, and at the last minute, grabbed her sketchbook. She headed down the hall, being careful not to look at the glass wall of the gallery, and left through the back door.

The swirling snow and strong wind stung Stella's cheeks as she unlocked her car and got inside. She sat in the driver's seat and stared straight ahead. She remembered a veteran professor telling her a story about the building being haunted, but Stella wasn't sure she believed in ghosts. Of course, she hadn't believed that her grandmother was alive in another world until four months ago. At this point, paranormal entities might as well be as real too.

Stella started the car and turned on the radio. The pop music that surrounded her took her mind off the mystery woman. The drive was less hectic than before; the snowplows had cleared the road and the traffic was not as heavy, but Stella still gripped the steering wheel hard, trying to concentrate on the road.

Roxanne greeted Stella as she walked through the front door. The cat's mews were ignored as Stella took off her coat and set her things down. It wasn't until Roxanne began clawing at her pant leg that Stella noticed her.

"Okay, okay. I'm happy to see you too." Stella picked up Roxanne and headed to the kitchen. She poured a small bowl of milk for Roxanne before making herself a peanut butter and jelly sandwich. Stella could feel her stomach settle as she chewed: one problem solved.

Stella made a cup of tea and went to the front door, where she found her sketchbook. She rummaged in her purse for her back-up pencil and made herself comfortable on the couch in the living room. Stella sipped on her tea as she turned the pages of her sketchbook until she came to her drawing of Jerot, the flat imitation. She flipped to the next page, which was blank.

Stella scratched away on the paper. The image of the blonde woman was beginning to come back. The image was so fleeting that Stella wasn't sure what she had been wearing, so she focused on the face. Stella became lost in her work, sketching and erasing and sketching more. She closed her eyes, desperate to remember that face. Who was she? Did Stella know her? Stella continued to draw, freeze-framing that instant on the page. The woman had narrow eyes and a slim nose. Stella detailed her full lips and the long hair that was sleek and beautiful. She was determined to capture every detail.

Stella had completed the face as best as she could, attaching the head to a slender neck and delicate shoulders. This woman would make a stunning sculpture. Stella finished the drawing before collapsing on the couch from exhaustion.

***

"Wake up, sleepy head," Ryan was leaning over her as Stella opened her eyes.

"What happened?" Stella said, not fully aware of her surroundings.

"I would say you were working too hard," Ryan picked up the sketchbook that had slid onto the floor. It was opened to the drawing of Jerot, "Who's this handsome man?"

"Oh, that's no one," Stella readjusted her glasses. Ryan flipped to the next page of the blonde woman.

"Going back to people, are we?"

"Just for today," Stella took the sketchbook and put it on the coffee table, "I should get dinner ready."

"How about pizza instead?" Ryan helped Stella to stand up and then kissed her.

"Pizza sounds good." Stella walked to the kitchen and grabbed the phone. Fifteen minutes later there was a knock at the front door. Stella paid the young delivery boy (with a large tip for coming out in the snow) and brought the pizza into the dining room. Stella always got a pizza with just green peppers; for some reason, that is all she liked on a pizza while Ryan was a bacon and onion fan.

"What's the plan for tonight?" Stella cut up her pizza with a fork and knife. She never ate pizza with her fingers. Ryan looked at her and gave her a raised eyebrow, causing Stella to giggle; she knew what that look meant.

After dinner, they retreated to bed and made love. Ryan was always gentle and passionate to Stella in the bedroom; they kissed and Stella closed her eyes; she couldn't help but envision it was Jerot making love to her. She couldn't help but wonder how his sexual technique was. She could imagine Jerot was rougher and had longer stamina. Was that wrong? Everyone fantasizes, don't they? When she and Ryan were both satisfied, they held each other in bed and talked.

"I love you," Ryan whispered into Stella's ear. She giggled like a teenager. Those three words made her forget all about the chilly weather, the mystery woman and even Jerot. Stella ran her fingers along Ryan's chest.

"I love you, too."

Ryan kissed Stella's neck, causing a new arousal between them. They made love a second time and no thought of Jerot crossed Stella's mind. She could only focus on the man before her and the pleasure he was making her feel. Exhausted, they lay in bed and Stella placed her head on her husband's shoulder.

"Never done that before."

"Impressive, no?" Ryan was still panting for air.

Stella chuckled; she could feel his shoulder move with the rhythm of his breathing. It lulled her into a faint sleep, until she could feel something poking at her foot. She looked up to see Roxanne, prodding at her feet; begging for attention.

"The cat wants food," Stella muttered.

"I'm on it," Ryan slid out of bed and put on a pair of sweatpants. He picked up Roxanne and went down to the kitchen. Stella got out of bed and put on her glasses and a pair of flannel pajamas. Though she was still warm, she knew the coldness outside would seep indoors. She looked in the mirror on her vanity and remembered the vision at the gallery, but no sign of the blonde woman appeared.

Stella walked into the kitchen finding Ryan boiling water in the teakettle on the stove.

"Hot chocolate?" he asked.

"Yes, please." Stella said. They settled on the couch and watched the evening news on television. Stella stared into her hot chocolate; the last time she drank this was with Jerot and a few villagers around the bonfire. She remembered Julie asking about them getting married and Jerot's reaction. Stella couldn't help but smile.

"You all right?" Ryan asked. "Not enough marshmallows?"

"Oh, no. It's fine," Stella sipped her drink. "Just waiting for it to cool a bit." She drank from her mug while the weatherman talked about an upcoming snowstorm.

"Great," muttered Ryan. "Vegas can't come soon enough." Stella leaned against her husband, his body heat and the hot chocolate made her sleepy again.

"I should go to bed," Stella said, finishing her drink. "I seem to be really sleepy today."

"Well, you should sleep in tomorrow," suggested Ryan. "You don't have anywhere to go, do you?"

"Not really. I could use some extra sleep," Stella kissed Ryan good night and put her mug in the kitchen sink; it can be washed tomorrow. She dragged herself back upstairs to the bedroom. Before she buried herself in the covers, Stella opened her small jewelry box and took out her grandmother's ring. She slipped it onto to her right ring finger, removed her glasses and jumped into bed, where she almost instantly fell asleep.

The Island

A massive snowstorm had trapped many of the villagers of Cobalian inside their homes and kept Stella inside the castle. She took the opportunity to wander the castle, discovering new things behind every door. Most of the rooms were empty and a few rooms were used as storage.

Stella strolled around in the library; the room filled with shelves upon shelves of books that she saw when she first came to the castle months ago. She scanned the shelves, but most of the books were old and full of historical records. Many books had been removed to the throne room, where Stella's grandmother was still searching for that piece of history she was keeping a secret.

Stella found the grand ballroom of the castle. The hardwood floor was made of walnut and the white walls were adorned with blue and white banners. A large fireplace was off to the side, and a mural of blue and white flowers decorated the vaulted ceiling.

One morning, Stella found a small room filled with several pieces of china. She looked at the beautiful white plates, each one trimmed with gold and painted with a single blue rose. These had to be for only the most important guests.

"Don't touch those," said a familiar voice, "or the Queen will have your hide made into a rug." Stella turned to see Jerot leaning against the doorway.

"I know better," Stella smiled. "Is it lunch time?"

"Yep," Jerot smiled, "we'd better hurry. I'm sure Mullitor's waiting for us." Every Friday, Stella and Jerot spent the afternoon with Mullitor. They would ride on the dragon's back as he flew them around Mayazure, showing Stella every part of the strange world. Stella's favorite place was Chamoisee Canyon, a rust-colored stone gorge that put the Grand Canyon to shame. The valley was so deep that you couldn't see the river at the bottom. Mullitor swore he had flown down far enough to see the river; he said it was shimmering silver and flowed tranquilly. Stella had never seen it, but she believed him.

Stella enjoyed lunch with her grandmother, Jerot and Tuptup. The dwarf made tomato soup with grilled sandwiches prepared with the finest of cheeses. Stella couldn't help but have seconds. When lunch was over, Jerot rose from his chair.

"Ready?" he asked Stella.

"I'll be down in a few," Stella pointed to her teacup. "I'm not finished yet."

"I'll get my horse ready and meet you outside." Stella watched as Jerot left. As soon as the silver door closed behind him, she turned to her grandmother and Tuptup.

"I have something to tell you," she said.

"What is it dear?" Queen Iona smiled, but her eyes showed worry.

"I won't be coming here for a week, starting on Tuesday. I'm going on vacation with Ryan to Las Vegas and I'm going to leave the ring at home so nothing bad happens to it. I'll be back before Christmas."

"Good for you," said Tuptup. "Everyone needs a vacation."

"Indeed," agreed Queen Iona. "And I think keeping my ring in a safe place is a good idea." Stella nodded.

"I take it Jerot doesn't know," Tuptup raised an eyebrow.

Stella sighed, "I haven't said anything yet. I know he'll be okay with not seeing me for a week, but the reason may upset him." Stella knew Jerot was jealous of Ryan, for he had what Jerot wanted. She always was careful not to mention her husband too often.

"He is still not over the fact that you look like Saura?" Queen Iona asked.

"No, it's worse." Stella looked down at her teacup. "He has now fallen for me. At least that's what he said."

"Hmm," Tuptup leaned back in her chair. "Perhaps the vacation will do him good as well."

Stella wrapped her cloak tightly around her as she came out through the main door of the castle. The snowstorm had stopped, but piles of snow were everywhere and the wind was still biting. Jerot waited with his Friesian at the end of the topaz walkway. They mounted the magnificent horse and trotted out of the city, heading north. They entered the snow-covered forest and continued on the snowy path towards the Cave of Eternal Blaze, where Mullitor lived.

Everything around them was white. The snow created an essence of purity and innocence to the forest. Stella was silent during the ride; she could tell Jerot now, they were alone. How would she tell him? She couldn't just blurt it out unexpectedly. She had to tread carefully so as not to hurt his feelings.

"You seem quiet," Jerot steered his horse through the snow. "Is everything all right?"

"Oh yes," Stella was unaware how long she had been day-dreaming, "I was just looking at the trees."

"Seem bare, don't they?"

"Yes," Stella said, "I think I like them better with leaves."

They made it to the foot of the large mountain. The gray sky and white snow made the mountain look almost black. They dismounted and Jerot tied his Friesian to a nearby tree; the horse dug through the snow with his nose, searching for something to chew on.

"Be good," Jerot patted the horse's shoulder. He took Stella by the hand and they walked up the rocky stairway to the cave. The steps were slippery with ice, but they made it to the outer ledge of the cave without incident.

Stella went through the gaping entrance of the cave, followed by

Jerot. The familiar darkness surrounded them, but it was no longer scary to her. She listened carefully for signs of life, but all that she heard was the blowing wind.

"Mullitor? You in here?" Stella called into the cave. She heard thunderous galloping from far inside the cave. Suddenly, the massive purple dragon appeared, stopping short of running Stella over.

"You're here!" Mullitor beamed with delight. He lowered his head to let Stella and Jerot hug him around his neck. Stella couldn't see it, but she could feel the vibrations of his tail beating frantically on the ground like a gigantic puppy, happy that his owner has come home. "I have something to show you. I think I may have discovered a new place in Mayazure."

"A new place?" asked Stella. "How exciting."

"Sounds like an adventure to me," Jerot said. He helped Stella climb onto Mullitor's back before scaling up himself. Stella grabbed Mullitor's mane as he went outside to the ledge.

"Ready?" Mullitor asked.

"I think so," Stella could feel Jerot tighten his arms around her waist. He wasn't as brave about flying as Stella was.

"Good, because we are going pretty high today," Mullitor spread his wings wide and in that instant, they were off the ground.

The brisk air lightly stung Stella and Jerot's cheeks. Mullitor turned his body to the northwest, his wings beating at the air in a steady rhythm. Stella looked down to see the world beneath them, it was a sea of white; every inch was covered in snow. Mullitor continued to ascend until he was above the clouds.

"Oh boy," Jerot squeezed Stella tighter. "You weren't kidding."

Mullitor laughed, "It will be well worth it." He soared above the clouds, his feet gently touching the white puffy haze beneath him. Stella looked forward, eager to see where they were going. It must be a mountainous peak they were going to. It couldn't be anything else, could it?

After several minutes of riding above the clouds, Stella saw a small dot in the distance. As they came closer, Stella was able to see it was an island, floating in the middle of nowhere. Mullitor circled around and lightly landed on the soft green grass growing on the hovering rock. It was just large enough to fit the three of them. Gladioli were growing in random patches and in the center of the island was a large flowering tree of purple blooms.

"It's so beautiful," was all Stella could say.

"Since it is above the clouds, there's no snow," said Mullitor. "In fact, it's too high up even for birds to get here. We might be the first ever to see this place."

"I think you're right," Jerot said. "I have never seen anything like this on any map."

Stella and Jerot slid off of Mullitor's back. Stella inched towards the end of the island and looked down. Through a small break in the clouds, she saw they had to be thousands of feet up in the air. Stella walked backwards away from the edge and latched on to the tree.

"This can't be safe," she said.

"Have no fear," Mullitor said. "If you fall, I will swoop down and catch you before you even know you fell off in the first place."

Stella sat down at the base of the tree. Its purple blossoms swayed in the light breeze. "I think I'll just stay right here."

"Good idea," Jerot said as he sat down next to Stella.

Mullitor sniffed the air. His eyes narrowed as he caught the scent of something. "You'll have to excuse me," he said, "I think I smell lunch." He spread his wings and took off into the clouds.

The island hovered motionless, hanging on an invisible string. Stella leaned against the tree and closed her eyes. The scent of the gladioli tickled her nose. Her fingers ran across the green grass and the wind howled faintly. It was a peaceful place, a perfect place.

"Stella," there was that tone again. She opened her eyes to see Jerot looking at her. She put a finger to her lips.

"Shhh," she whispered. "Let's just relax a bit, okay?"

"I'll relax when I'm asleep. We are alone." Jerot took Stella's hand, "I care about you deeply. I long to kiss you."

"Jerot, please." Stella felt uncomfortable. What if Mullitor caught them? He would surely fricassee Jerot in a heartbeat. Stella decided she had to tell him about her vacation now, before they began this daily battle. "I need to tell you something."

"Please do," Jerot said, expectantly. Her words caught him off guard.

"Starting Tuesday, I won't be coming here. I'm going on vacation with…," Stella hesitated, "with Ryan to a place called Las Vegas. But I promise I'll be back before Christmas."

"I see," Jerot looked away from her. He stood and walked towards the edge of the floating island. For a moment, Stella thought he was going to jump, but he just stood there with his back to her. "You are choosing him over me, again," he said, not turning around.

Stella stood up and walked towards Jerot. She placed her hand on his shoulder, but he didn't look at her. "Ryan is my husband. You are my friend. Maybe a little time apart will help you see that," she said.

Jerot turned towards her, his eyes desperately holding back tears. "When will it be my turn?" he asked, "When will you do something with me?"

"I do lots of things with you," Stella said, insulted by his words, "I could just hang out with grandma and Tuptup all day, if you'd rather I do that."

"That's not what I meant."

"Oh?" Stella placed her hands on her hips. "Explain then."

"I mean," Jerot paused, trying to find the words. "When will you love me? When will you spend time with me because you love me?"

Stella looked at the ground. She couldn't think of an answer. She did love him, but she couldn't be unfaithful to Ryan. "I'm afraid I don't have an answer."

"I know," Jerot touched her cheek. "it's okay. I understand. I just feel saddened that you won't be here. I'm just being selfish."

"It's only for a week," Stella's defenses had subsided the moment his fingers touched her skin. "We'll spend Christmas together and will have lots of fun and holiday cheer. I promise."

Mullitor returned, with blood-stained claws. Fortunately, he had eaten his lunch before coming back. "It's quite enjoyable up here, isn't it?"

"Oh yes. I could spend all day here," Stella said as she watched Mullitor clean his claws with his tongue. She felt a slight urge to vomit.

"I will have to tell the Queen about this place," Jerot said, "It is one of her duties to name the newly-discovered areas of Mayazure."

"I think the island should be named after me," said Mullitor. "I found it."

"I bet we could suggest that," Stella said. "I have a few ideas of my own."

The trio spent the rest of the afternoon on the peaceful island. Stella had to remove her cloak after a while, since the cold weather didn't reach the floating rock. With the help of Jerot's sword, Stella cut some gladioli to take back to her grandmother. She selected one stalk each of yellow, white and purple. As the sun began to sink towards the horizon, Mullitor took Stella and Jerot back to the Cave of Eternal Blaze.

"I will see you again next week?" Mullitor nuzzled Stella's shoulder with his snout.

"I'm afraid not," Stella said. "I'm going to take a week break from Mayazure. I'm going on a trip with Ryan, so I'm leaving the ring at home where it will be safe."

"I will miss you," Mullitor's green eyes were sad. "But I think leaving the ring in a safe place is a good idea. I wouldn't know how to live if you didn't return."

"Neither would I," muttered Jerot, causing Stella to blush.

"You two functioned well without me before," Stella ran her fingers over the soft fur of Mullitor's neck. "Don't worry, I will return."

"That was a different time. It was before we knew you," Jerot said.

"Well, just pretend it is that different time and, before you know it, I'll be back."

"You are right," Mullitor said. "It's not forever."

"Exactly," Stella smiled. "Besides, what could possibly change in a week?'

Once they said their goodbyes to Mullitor, Stella and Jerot mounted his Friesian and made their way back to Cobalian. The ride back was even quieter than before. Neither of them spoke until they were in the city.

"Are you sure you have to go?" Jerot asked as he stabled his horse. "Can't you cancel it?"

Stella drew a line in the snow with her foot. It wasn't perfectly straight. She would like to find someone who could do it. "I can't just cancel it. I have already paid for the hotel and the plane tickets."

"I will pay you double if you cancel."

Stella smiled, "I can't take your money with me. You know that."

They walked their way through the snow and up into the castle, to the throne room. The Queen was thumbing through another library book, while Tuptup set the mahogany table for dinner.

"How was this afternoon with Mullitor?" asked Queen Iona as she closed her book and placed it on top of a pile of others.

"It was wonderful," Stella couldn't contain her excitement. "Mullitor discovered a floating island. I picked some flowers for you too."

"Oh, how wonderful and those flowers are beautiful."

"I'll take those," said Tuptup, taking the gladioli. "I have just the vase for them," and he waddled to the gold door leading to the Den, and disappeared.

"So where is this island?" asked Queen Iona.

"To the Northwest," said Jerot. "We were pretty high up, but I reckon we were close to the Goblin city of Wreckton."

"Fascinating."

"Can you name it after Mullitor?" Stella asked, "we could call it Dragon Island since nothing can reach it but a dragon."

"Perhaps," Queen Iona said. "I'll think while we eat."

Dinner consisted of smoked ham with potatoes and carrots, sliced apples with honey and lemon meringue pie for desert. Stella and Jerot took turns telling Tuptup and the Queen about the island; how high it was, the tree with the purple blossoms and how the cold weather didn't even reach it. The Queen ate silently, listening to everything, while Tuptup asked questions.

"Well," Tuptup dipped his fork into the pie, "I think it sounds almost as great as the Welcome Garden. In fact, I think it should be called the Welcome Island. Seems to be a nice match."

"No, I like Dragon Island better," said Stella. "It's more suitable."

"I agree," chimed in Jerot.

"You would," Tuptup gave him a sly smile.

"I think it should be called Mullitor's Island," said Queen Iona and, just like that, it was settled.

"Oh," said Stella, "Mullitor will be so pleased."

The Queen nodded. "Of course. He is the last dragon and I think having his name on something will leave a legacy for generations to come. He deserves such an honor. Tuptup, can you get me the declaration papers? We need to make this official."

Stella watched as her grandmother wrote on the same parchments she had seen before: The fancy blue border, the *Royal Declaration of Queen Iona of Cobalian, Capital of Mayazure* at the top of the page, with the seal below. The Queen passed the parchment over to Stella for her to read.

> *It has been informed to Queen Iona of Cobalian that a new land in the form of a floating island has been discovered northwest of the city of Wreckton. Queen Iona hereby names the new land* Mullitor's Island *in honor of Mullitor the dragon, who discovered it.*
>
> *Signed,*
> *Queen Iona Bale Of Cobalian, Mayazure*

"It's wonderful," Stella said, giving it her verbal seal of approval. Tuptup stamped the parchment with a wax seal while the Queen wrote out more copies.

"We can go see him tomorrow to tell him the news," Jerot said to Stella.

"Oh, that would be a superb surprise," Stella was full of excitement.

"It is my Christmas present to him," said Queen Iona. "Hopefully he won't return it." Everyone laughed.

Tuptup gathered all the copies except one. He rolled it up and tied it with a blue silk ribbon and handed it to Jerot. "Since you are going to see Mullitor again tomorrow, have him take you to the island so you can post this on the blossom tree."

"Will do," Jerot said.

"I will have these sent to every corner of Mayazure," Tuptup said as he left the throne room.

Stella helped Jerot clear the mahogany table of the dinnerware while her grandmother picked up another book. When she entered the Den with a stack of dirty dishes, the room was a large kitchen with little troll-like creatures washing and drying and putting away the dishes. Stella had never seen these creatures before; they were quite cute.

"Who are these creatures?" Stella asked Jerot while she passed her dishes to a waiting troll.

"They are Minots, or pygmy trolls"

"Oh, these aren't…" Stella paused, but Jerot understood.

"No," he said. "The trolls that attacked us long ago are a different breed. They are distantly related to the Minots, but not as nice."

"Oh good," Stella watched the Minots work. "These guys are too cute to be invaders. They're not slaves, are they?" Stella would never think her grandmother would own slaves.

"Of course not," Jerot smiled. "They are paid to care for the castle and do any odd jobs the Queen needs. We would never enslave anyone."

"Well, that's good."

Stella and Jerot left the Minots to their work and joined Queen Iona in the throne room. Stella picked up one of the books and saw that a chapter was marked. She flipped to it and noticed it was about portals and cross-dimensional theories. This definitely wasn't history, as her grandmother had mentioned before.

"What exactly are you looking for?" Stella asked.

"Ah, that is a secret," Queen Iona took the book from Stella and placed it back on the pile. "Besides, I'm not really sure what I'm looking for."

"How can you be looking for something if you don't even know what it is?" Jerot asked the question before Stella could.

The Queen simply chuckled. "I'll know it when I find it," was all she said.

Stella and Jerot spent the evening playing cards. Jerot tried to teach her Givlok, which was much like Gin Rummy, but with a few added rules. Stella would get frustrated when she thought she had a good hand, but then didn't because of one strange rule or another. She was relieved when it was finally late enough for Jerot had to leave. She walked down the spiral staircase with Jerot and in the foyer, Jerot spoke.

"My offer still stands. I'll pay you double to stay."

"I would, but if I lost the ring while on vacation, I will never see you again." Stella said.

"You won't lose it."

"I am not taking that risk," Stella wrapped her arms around Jerot. "Let's make the best of the few days we have before I go. We'll see Mullitor tomorrow and have a whole weekend of fun."

Jerot returned the embrace. "Okay, I will see you tomorrow" he said. They looked at each other for a moment before Jerot let Stella go for the night.

The Vacation

Stella shoved and pushed at her carry-on bag, trying to squeeze it into the overhead compartment on the airplane, but no luck. The wheels on the bottom of the bag may make it easy to drag around, but they added a few inches that made it too large to fit.

"Come on, you piece of crap," Stella continued to jam the bag.

"Let me do it," Ryan chimed in, his bag easily in place. With every ounce of strength, he gave the bag a massive thrust and then quickly slammed the compartment door shut.

"Thank you," Stella said, finally able to sit down. The plane was nothing like a dragon. Stale air circulated in the cabin instead of fresh air blowing in your face. Everything was metal and plastic. Dragons didn't have turbulence or expensive drinks or tiny windows you could barely see out of. Mullitor's rides were smooth, and the views were always breathtaking. This wasn't an exciting adventure; this was more like a flying can of human sardines.

Ryan sat down next to Stella and took her hand. "Are we having fun yet?" Ryan loved to fly, but he's never flown quite like Stella has.

"Tons," Stella rolled her eyes and clicked the button to turn on the fan. All it did was blow the air around, with no feeling of freshness. Once everyone was seated, the flight attendants did their routine of showing where the exits were and how to use the life jackets, as if they were even flying over any oceans. Stella found the whole safety procedure thing uncomfortable and pointless. If they were going to crash, they were going to die; it's just fact. It was also a fact that Mullitor would never crash; he had more control over his body than the pilots had control of the plane. One malfunctioning part and down they go. Stella tightened her seatbelt like it would be her saving grace.

After the flight attendants did their skit, they sealed and locked the airplane doors and the plane began to taxi to its predestine runway. Stella squeezed Ryan's hand as the plane gathered speed. She could feel the instant the tires of the plane left the ground and immediately felt sick. She closed her eyes as the plane rose upwards above the clouds. When the plane leveled out, she opened her eyes.

"That wasn't so bad," Ryan smiled and Stella returned the favor. The pilot's voice came over the intercom announcing that the flight was on schedule and that it was a nice seventy degrees Fahrenheit in Las Vegas. The flight attendants returned to get drink orders and to pass out headphones for watching the movie or listening to the radio. Stella took a pair and ordered a soda while Ryan decided to pass on the movie, but ordered a Screwdriver.

***

The plane circled the Las Vegas airport before it began its descend. Stella gripped Ryan's arm; landing was more frightening for her than taking off, because they were basically doing a planned, safe version of a slow crash. If anything went wrong, it would all be over for everyone. She kept glancing out the window to see the tiny houses and buildings getting bigger as they got closer to the runway. Stella wanted to look so she knew exactly when they would hit the ground, but didn't want to look for fear they might be going down too fast. Once Stella could make out the vehicles zooming on their tiny roads, she closed the blind. The plane landed with a slight bump, followed by a rapid deceleration. Stella let out a sigh of relief.

Once off the plane, Ryan and Stella made their way to baggage claim. They walked past rows of slot machines between terminals. You knew you were in Vegas when there were slot machines at the airport. Stella felt the slight anxiety at the baggage claim. What if her luggage was lost? Stella didn't want to imagine all her clothes gone in luggage limbo, never to be seen again. After waiting patiently for fifteen minutes, Ryan and Stella spotted their matching suitcases travel down the conveyor belt; another hurdle successfully jumped.

Ryan hailed a taxi and the driver helped load up the luggage into the trunk, "Where to?" asked the driver.

"The Venetian," said Ryan. The Venetian hotel and casino was a beautiful building with an Italian theme. It even had canals filled with water flowing inside the building, complete with gondolas. It was one of the most romantic hotels in Vegas.

"You picked a great time to come to Vegas," the driver said. "Not too hot, not too cold and full of great places to do last-minute holiday shopping."

"Good," Stella said. "I haven't done one bit of Christmas shopping." The driver chuckled. They pulled up to the Venetian and a bellhop greeted them. He was a young man with black hair; he looked like a young Jerot. Ryan paid the driver before helping the bellhop with the bags. Stella watched people enjoying the gondola rides; that was something she and Ryan would have to try later.

After checking in, the bellhop helped carry the luggage up to their room on the sixth floor. Ryan tipped the bellhop and once he was gone, both Stella and Ryan collapsed onto the king size bed.

"Ugh," Stella felt exhausted.

Ryan turned to her, "Room Service?"

"Yes," Stella glanced at the clock on the nightstand and saw it was way past the dinner hour. "I'm too tired to even think about going out."

Ryan grabbed the phone and ordered two mushroom cheeseburgers, a pint tub of coleslaw and a bottle of red wine. Within twenty minutes, the food had arrived. Stella dived into the coleslaw while Ryan picked some of the lettuce out of his burger, "They always put too much on."

"You just don't like it to begin with," Stella said. After eating, Ryan popped open the wine and they celebrated their successful arrival. They got somewhat tipsy, and went to bed for love-making, which the alcohol made awkward.

Ryan soon fell asleep after trying his best to drunkenly please his wife. Stella laid in bed, staring at the ceiling. This would be her first complete night's sleep in four months without the ring. She would have dreams that weren't real and nightmares that seemed too real. She wished she had taken the ring with her. She turned to Ryan, "You awake?" Ryan just grunted. "I'm gonna go down and play the slot machines, okay?"

Ryan managed a sleepy reply. "Okay."

Stella dressed and left the room, heading toward the elevator. Ryan was a whiz when it came to blackjack or roulette, but Stella just stuck to the slot machines. Watching the wheels spin gave her all the entertainment she needed. Stella wandered between the slot machines on the casino floor. Every machine had its own colorful theme, fantasy, historical, or just plain weird. Stella stopped at one that had a large purple dragon on it; that was a sign, if she ever saw one.

Stella put in a twenty-dollar bill and began to play. If she got three dragons, she earned an extra spin, three of any kind meant she doubled her bet. Fifteen minutes into the game, a waitress dressed like a sexy Roman goddess approached Stella. "Would you like a drink?"

"Oh yes," Stella smiled, "I would just like a Manhattan, please." The young waitress left and returned shortly with Stella's drink. Stella reached into her pocket. "How much?"

"All drinks are free on the floor," said the waitress.

"Well, you still need a tip," and Stella gave the sexy Roman goddess two dollars.

"Thank you," she said.

"And thank you," Stella said before taking a sip.

After an hour at the slot machine, Stella finally gambled the last of the twenty dollars she had put in. She made up for it by having three Manhattans. She decided it was time to call it a night. She managed to stumble into the elevator and hit the button for the sixth floor.

The elevator had four walls of mirrors, which made Stella dizzy, looking at four drunken reflections of herself. She leaned against the back wall of the elevator as it rose. The opposite wall imitated Stella leaning in an intoxicated manner as it should and then she saw it: the blonde woman's face flashed past Stella's shoulder. The sudden ghostly image of the woman smacked the haze of the alcohol out of her. Stella turned, was she there? No. Stella looked all around, but saw nothing but her own reflection.

"No more alcohol," Stella said to herself as the doors opened to her floor. "I can't afford seeing things that aren't there. People will think I'm crazy."

***

Stella spent the next day sitting by the pool while Ryan braved the cold water. It was a pleasant seventy degrees, but the pool wasn't heated. Stella relaxed in a lounge chair in shorts and a t-shirt, wearing prescription sunglasses. The mysterious blonde woman was far from Stella's mind.

"You sure you don't want to join me?" Ryan called out from the deep end.

"Positive. I don't feel like freezing," Stella said.

"It's not that cold."

Stella reached into her bag and pulled out a stack of papers and a series of photographs. The essays were part of the final project she had assigned to her students, along with the photographs of each of their sculptures. Stella took one picture and turned it over to read the student's name written on the back. She then filed through the essays until she found the one written by the same student.

Stella looked at the photograph of the sculpture. It was a wood carving of a man from the waist up. His hands were on top of his head, ready to pull out his hair. The man's face was contorted in anger and frustration. Stella read the essay; about how the man reacted when he found out his brother had died in gang-related violence, after he had tried so hard to convince his brother to leave the gang, as he had done. Good story, good sculpture.

"Stop working, you're on vacation," Ryan said, now sitting in the lounge chair next to Stella.

"I'm just scanning a few so I don't have to work so hard when we get back." She could see the goosebumps on Ryan's arms. "I see you got cold enough."

"Eh, you can only swim for so long before you get tired," Ryan rubbed a beach towel over his body. "Wanna go Christmas shopping after dinner?"

"Sure. Let me just go over a few more of these before we go," Stella said, returning to the photos.

Once Ryan's suit was dry and Stella had worked long enough, they headed up to their room. Stella changed into a flowing purple skirt with a matching top while Ryan wore jeans and a black polo shirt.

"Let's go to that French restaurant downstairs. It looks good," Stella suggested.

"Hope they don't need reservations," Ryan said, grabbing his wallet.

As it happened, the restaurant did need a reservation, but the wait time for walk-ins was only thirty minutes. After getting their table, a short waiter with curly blonde hair approached them.

"Welcome," he said, "I'm John and I'll be your waiter. What can I get you to drink?"

"We would like a bottle of your sweetest blush wine," Ryan ordered and John vanished while Stella glanced over the menu.

"What looks good?" Ryan asked.

"Oh, it all looks good," Stella smiled. "I think I'll get this roasted chicken."

"What, no escargots?" Ryan gave a sly smile.

"Yuck, no."

John returned with the bottle of wine and poured two glasses. "Have we decided on what we are having?" Stella ordered the roasted chicken while Ryan decided on the prime rib. "I'll have those out in no time," and he again vanished.

"Where do you want to go shopping?" Ryan asked.

"Let's go to the Forum Shops in Caesar's Palace," Stella bounced excitedly in her seat. "I heard they have wonderful things there."

"Probably expensive too."

"Well, we were planning on spending a fortune on Christmas presents. Might as well be on designer things," Stella sipped her wine; it was sweet and went down easy.

The roasted chicken was exquisite and Ryan's prime rib was succulent, although more food than either of them thought it would be.

"I might need help with this," Ryan said.

"I don't know. I might be too full to help you," Stella cut up her chicken and ate heartily.

"Are there any shows you want to see while we are here?"

Stella chewed as she thought of an answer, "I probably would just want to see something here. No sense running around the Strip."

"I'll have to see what's going on here at the Venetian. I think there's a brochure in the hotel room."

The rest of the meal was eaten in silence; the food was too good to stop and chitchat. Ryan only ate half of his meal and asked John to pack up the rest in a box to take back to the room, although Stella managed to eat all of her roasted chicken. After a short trip to the hotel room to drop off Ryan's prime rib, he and Stella left the Venetian and decided to walk to the Forum Shops.

The weather was mild and pleasant to walk out in. Street performers were out and about, doing their job to entertain passersby merely for a tip. In just a short walk, Stella and Ryan passed a juggler, four Elvis impersonators and a unicycle-riding clown.

The Forum Shops at Caesar's Palace were spectacular. Roman columns and statues were everywhere. Stella and Ryan mainly window shopped but, before the evening was over, Stella had managed to buy a designer jacket for her dad, a beautiful blouse for her mom, a designer purse for her Aunt Shelly and cologne for her Uncle Dominic. Ryan bought a sausage and cheese gift basket for his dad, but had yet to decide on what to buy for the rest of his family.

"They're all so picky," Ryan said, as Stella paid for her mom's new blouse. "They never tell me what they want."

"Well, at these prices, they'd better like whatever you get them," Stella said.

When they finally made it back to the Venetian, it was late and Stella was tired. After carefully placing all of her gifts in her suitcase, she changed into a t-shirt and boxer shorts to wear to sleep.

"You're not going to go gambling with me?" asked Ryan.

"I'm just exhausted from all the shopping," Stella said as she washed her face in the bathroom sink. "Maybe tomorrow."

"Well, I'm feeling lucky. I'll just be gone for an hour or so," Ryan kissed his wife before leaving to go down to the casino floor.

Stella plopped into bed and turned on the television. She found a good movie and settled into the comfortable bed. The mattress was soft and the sheets weren't scratchy or stiff. Within a few minutes, she was asleep.

The mysterious blonde women crouched over the body of Jerot, who was lying on the floor. She was very thin and dressed in a deep red gown. Her hands were wrapped around

Jerot's neck, choking him vigorously. Jerot clawed at her hands and forearms, desperately trying to release the woman's grasp. His legs kicked the air, struggling to breathe. The woman cackled manically; she was too strong for Jerot. His face began to turn blue, his grip was losing power and his legs began to stop kicking. The woman increased her hold on his throat, shaking the life out of him.

"Stop!" Stella heard herself shout, causing herself to wake up. She quickly sat up in bed and saw the television was off, and Ryan sleeping next to her. Her glasses were buried in the sheets, so she put them on the nightstand. How long had she been asleep? Sweat poured from her face as she sat there, breathing rapidly, as if the blonde woman had been choking her. Stella buried her face in her hands. Was it really a dream or was someone from Mayazure trying to reach her for help? Why did she leave the ring at home? What if something was happening and she wasn't there to help? Stella placed her head on her pillow and stared at the ceiling. The rest of the night she worried and it wasn't until the first signs of dawn did she fall back asleep.

***

"Wake up, sleepy head," Stella rolled over to see Ryan leaning over her.

"What time is it?" Stella sat up and put on her glasses.

"Almost noon."

"Why did you let me sleep so late?"

"I couldn't help it," Ryan smiled, "You looked so peaceful. Now, get dressed so we can go to lunch. I'm hungry."

"Me too," Stella got dressed in a fresh shirt and jeans. She tried not to think about the dream. It couldn't be real because she didn't wear the ring. *I'm just imagining things*, she thought.

Ryan and Stella ate lunch at one of the Italian bistros before heading to the casino floor. Ryan chose a roulette table while Stella decided on the slot machines again.

"I'll check on you when I'm out of money," Stella said kissing Ryan on the cheek.

"Okay, I feel lucky today, so I should have more when you get here," Ryan chuckled.

Stella picked an Egyptian-themed slot machine this time, near a group of other machines in the corner of the casino. No one was using them and Stella felt like being alone, so she sat down at the machine. She put in her usual twenty dollars and began to place bets. Thirty minutes passed before she lost all the money and decided she had had enough of watching the wheels spin.

She headed back to the roulette table where Ryan was. Stella didn't understand exactly how it worked, but Ryan had indeed been lucky: he had about $200 worth of chips in front of him.

"Hey, back already?" he asked.

"Yeah, the slot machines weren't kind to me."

"Wanna help me pick some numbers?" Ryan pointed to the table.

"Um…" Stella paused. "The black twenty-two looks good."

"Let's bet that whole row," Ryan put a $5 chip the black twenty-two, as well as on the red twenty-three and the black twenty-four.

When all the bets where placed, the dealer spin the roulette wheel. The small white ball bounced and danced as it was spun around. Once the wheel finally stopped the dealer called out the winning number.

"Red fourteen."

"Dang," Ryan said. "Oh well, I was getting tired away," and he decided to cash out.

"Sorry I'm such a bad luck charm," Stella said.

"Don't worry about it," Ryan said, "I doubled my money, so it's all good. Hey, let's go for a gondola ride."

"Okay."

They chose a gondola on the canal inside of the hotel, where the line was shorter. The gondola driver sang romantic songs as they floated under bridges of onlookers.

"It is good luck to kiss your love as you go under a bridge," the driver said. Ryan complied and kissed Stella, making her giggle. The water lapped at the side of the gondola and they could see tiny fish swimming along the bottom of the canal. It was the most romantic part of the whole trip.

***

Before either of them knew it, the week was over and it was time to go home. Stella was glad to get home and spend the next night in Mayazure, instead of just sleeping. She'd kept having dreams about the mysterious blonde woman. Sometimes she would see the woman torturing someone she knew from Cobalian, but most of the time Stella just saw her laughing hysterically. Whoever she was, Stella sure didn't want to meet her.

The plane ride was smooth, but Stella couldn't wait to get off the plane. The whole flight, she daydreamed she was flying with Mullitor. She couldn't wait to feel the wind in her face and his mane between her fingers as she gripped tightly. She could only imagine the wonderful places he would take Stella next. *Dragons were definitely a better way to fly*, she thought.

Stella's mother, Celeste, was waiting for them in the main lobby of the airport. It was cheaper to get a ride than leave the car at the airport parking lot for a week. After the welcome home hugs and kisses, the three of them headed to the parking lot where Ryan and Stella stowed their luggage in the trunk of Celeste's car. Stella sat in the front passenger seat while Ryan spread himself out in the back.

"How was the trip?" Celeste asked as she started the car,

"It was great," Stella said. "We saw some great shows and even got all our Christmas shopping done."

"Did you win anything?"

"I didn't, but Ryan won about $500. How's Roxanne?"

"Oh, she's fine," Celeste and Stella's father, Ferdinand, had been taking care of the cat while Ryan and

Stella were gone. "I'm sure she'll be glad to see you."

"I'll be glad to she her," said Ryan. "I miss my princess."

"You spoil her like a child," Celeste said. Stella gave her a look; *please don't start asking about grandkids*, she thought. Stella flipped on the radio to prevent any conversation about babies before it got started.

Celeste was right: as soon as they walked in the front door, Roxanne was at Stella's feet, begging for attention. Stella scooped up the cat and gave her a hug and a kiss on the forehead, "How's my little baby?" asked Stella.

"I knew she missed you," said Celeste. Roxanne purred as Stella passed the tricolor fluffball to Ryan. He kissed Roxanne and cradled her in his arms.

"Thanks for the ride," said Stella as she hugged her mother.

"You're welcome. Glad to see you are home."

After Celeste left, Stella opened a can of cat food and while Roxanne ate, Ryan and Stella unpacked. Ryan called the local sandwich restaurant to have two subs delivered to the house. They ate in peace and quiet of the old Victorian house they called home.

Stella chewed while she thought of Mayazure. She couldn't wait to see her grandmother and Tuptup, Jerot and Mullitor. She couldn't wait to tell them about the wonderful week she'd had. She missed them terribly and felt empty without her nighttime visits. She could imagine she missed all sorts of wonderful things while she was gone.

After dinner, Stella washed the few dishes while Ryan dried them. Then they relaxed on the couch with Roxanne and enjoyed the numbing effect of the television. There was nothing good to watch, but Ryan found a decent science show while Stella just peacefully rested her head on Ryan's shoulder.

"I think I'm going to go to bed," Stella yawned.

"Now? It's kinda early," Ryan said.

"I know, but that plane ride wore me out." This was true, but Stella also couldn't wait any longer to get to Mayazure.

"You're right. Maybe I will go to bed soon as well." Ryan sighed. "Gotta go back to work."

"Same here," Stella stood up causing Roxanne to fall off her lap. "I have to grade those sculptures so I can report the grades before the deadline." Stella kissed Ryan good night and headed up the stairs to the bathroom. She washed her face and changed into her flannel pajamas.

Before hopping into bed, Stella opened her small silver jewelry box to find her grandmother's ring, waiting for her. It looked duller than usual. "Maybe I should have this cleaned," Stella spoke to herself, and she slipped the ring onto her right hand. She removed her glasses and got into bed. The cool sheets and soft mattress relaxed her, but she was too excited to sleep. Roxanne jumped on the bed and curled into a ball next to Stella. She ran her hand over the soft fur of her cat, who purred happily. Stella could only stare at the ceiling; she just couldn't sleep.

After a while, Ryan came into the bedroom. "Can't sleep?"

"I thought I was tired, but I guess not," Stella said.

"I can think of something to tire you out," Ryan winked making Stella chuckle.

"I really am not in the mood for sex."

Ryan changed into a pair of boxer shorts and hopped into bed. Roxanne was forced to move to the foot of the bed, which she protested by hissing. Ryan held Stella in his arms; this always made Stella sleepy. The way he held her was so comfortable and inviting that she couldn't help but relax into a deep sleep.

The Message

Stella could smell the flowers of the Welcome Garden before she could see them. She opened her eyes to see all the flowers as usual, in all their eternal springtime glory. A faint breeze caused the flowers to sway rhythmically, as if they were waving a friendly greeting to her.

Stella turned to the entrance of the garden, expecting Jerot to be there as always, but he wasn't there. *Maybe he lost track of time*, Stella thought. He must have just forgotten what day she was returning.

As she stepped out of the garden and into the forest, the reality of winter hit Stella, making her shiver. A new layer of snow lay on the ground, covering the forest and the brick path. Stella wrapped her arms around herself and proceeded down the walkway. She made it to the fork in the road and without a second thought, turned left. The bare trees of the forest did not protect Stella from the chilling wind; she could feel her teeth begin to chatter from the cold. This made her walk faster for, not only did she want to see everyone, but now she wanted to be warm.

Stella was halfway down the snow-covered path when she heard a rustling from a nearby bush. She stopped in her tracks; what was that? A squirrel? A deer? A troll? Stella watched as the bush rattled and shook, and then a short man with long red hair came tumbling out.

"Tuptup!" Stella helped the dwarf to his feet. "What are you doing out here?"

"Shh!" Tuptup raised a finger to his lips. "We have to be quiet. I'm glad I caught you before you got too close to Cobalian."

"Why? What's at Cobalian?" Tuptup didn't answer Stella's questions.

"Here," Tuptup gave Stella a cloak to put on. "Follow me," and he started off into the woods. They walked a distance of twenty feet before walking parallel to the brick path. "They sometimes patrol the path, so we have to go this way."

"Who?" Stella asked as she tiptoed behind Tuptup. Again he raised a finger to his lips as they neared the opening to the grand city of Cobalian. Through the trees, Stella could see the wall, but it was no longer brilliant white; it was shrouded in gray and the golden gate was dull and hung crooked on its hinges. In front of the gate were two minotaurs, creatures with the body of a human, but with the head of a bull. They guarded the entrance with long spears and shields. "What are those?"

"Come on," Tuptup said. "The Queen is waiting for you." They walked northward through the woods until they came upon the path towards the Cave of Eternal Blaze. Stella began to worry and was irritated by the fact that Tuptup wasn't answering her questions.

"Is she okay?" Stella asked.

"Oh yes, she's as fine as she's going to be," Tuptup said without looking back at Stella, as they passed Bondi Field. She thought about asking where Jerot was, but decided against it.

They made it to the Cave of Eternal Blaze, dark as always. Stella climbed up the stone stairway while Tuptup struggled slightly. Once inside the cave, Tuptup grabbed a lantern near the entrance and lit it. He led the way through the dark tunnel to the cavern inside, where now rested all the souls of deceased dragons. With the lantern, Stella could see where she was going for the first time. The walls of the tunnel glimmered with dew, and the floor was a dusty dirt floor.

Stella was surprised by what the cavern revealed: It opened up before her and it was as if the whole city of Cobalian had packed up and moved in. Each family had their own nook, and a section of the massive cavern had turned into the trade quarter. Children ran this way and that, enjoying the flickering crystals in the cavern.

"What's going on?" Stella asked in shock.

"Perhaps I can answer that," said a voice to Stella's right. It was her grandmother, walking towards her. The townspeople bowed as she past them, but she gave them no acknowledgement. Stella hugged her grandmother in greeting, who then continued. "While you were gone, Cobalian was captured by the Princess of Sinopia."

"Sinopia?" Stella was surprised; she had never heard of this place.

"Well, actually, Sinopia is in ruins now," Queen Iona said. "You know the fork in the road? Well, if you turn to the right, you'll run into what's left of Sinopia."

"But I wouldn't suggest it," Tuptup added.

"Why? What happened?" Stella had so many questions.

"Perhaps you need some history," Queen Iona sat down on a large boulder and Stella joined her. "After the failed invasion by the trolls ten years ago, the trolls moved east to the neighboring city of Sinopia, which was not as lucky as we were. It was said no one survived, but we were wrong. A young girl named Stella Cinereous, also known as the Princess of Sinopia, managed to escape."

"Another Stella," Stella said. "How interesting."

"I prefer her other name," said Tuptup. "Stella the Subjugator. Just don't say it to her face."

"Yes, a total coincidence," said Queen Iona ignoring Tuptup. "For ten years she has been hiding in secret, building an army to come and take our city. Most of us escaped, the rest were captured as slaves."

Those last words worried Stella. Jerot was nowhere to be seen. She wanted to ask if he was one of the captured, but a more important question had to be asked first, "Why would she attack a neighboring city?"

"Jealousy," Tuptup muttered. "She was a spoiled brat when she was a child and she's a spoiled brat now."

"Yes," Queen Iona added. "She wouldn't dare try to take back Sinopia; it is too far gone. She wanted a city to rule and Cobalian was the best choice."

Stella couldn't contain her worry, and finally asked, "Where's Jerot?"

"Oh, he's dealing with more important business," Queen Iona smiled. "He took Mullitor to Wreckton to gain allies and get supplies from the goblins."

"So we're going to fight back?"

"It hasn't been decided yet," Tuptup said. "We can't just go and attack; we are more civilized than that. A battle plan must be worked on."

"It may take a few days, even weeks, but we will fight to get Cobalian back," said Queen Iona.

The conversation flooded Stella's thoughts. She had so many other questions to ask, but her brain was still trying to absorb all this information. "I think I need a walk," she said.

"You do that," said Queen Iona, "I have matters to discuss with my spy," she winked at Tuptup.

Stella walked through the cavern, passing makeshift campsites of civilians. For an exiled bunch, they seemed happy. She managed to walk out, beyond all the people, and found a small nook of her own. The crystals sparkled and cast her reflection as she walked past them. She knelt down to look at a shimmering red crystal. It glowed faintly as she stared into it, deep in thought. She felt horrible, almost guilty. Why had she left the ring at home? She should have been here to help fight. Tears filled her eyes; she was so ashamed of her absence.

"There you are," Stella turned to see that Jerot had entered the nook where she rested. "I have been looking for you. Are you all right?" he asked.

"I was about to ask you the same thing," Stella wiped her eyes with the sleeve of her sweater. She stood and hugged Jerot tightly. He squeezed her back.

"I have missed you so much," Jerot whispered into Stella's ear.

"Same here," Stella answered. They looked at each other. Jerot touched her cheek with his fingers. He leaned in to kiss her and Stella pulled away. "No."

"But I haven't seen you for a week," Jerot took a step forward and Stella stepped back to stay out of his reach.

"I don't care if it's been a year. It just isn't right."

"Please?" again Jerot moved forward. Stella was trapped in the nook of the cavern, nearly pinned against the wall.

In her panic she tripped over a yellow crystal and fell backwards. Jerot tried to catch her, but he wasn't fast enough. Stella landed on her back, her arm scraping against a pink crystal, cutting her sweater and gouging a deep cut into her left forearm. She cried out in pain. In a flash, Jerot ripped off his tunic and tore it to make a bandage. For the first time, Stella saw his bare chest. For a man in his forties, his muscles were well toned. Stella felt herself blushing; she couldn't stop looking at him. She was finally distracted when Jerot took her arm, which hurt. He began to wrap Stella's arm with his shredded tunic.

"Oh my God, I'm so sorry," he repeated over and over again. His words agitated Stella; she wished he would stop saying that. "I'm so sorry, please forgive me," he continued. Finally Stella slapped him across the face with her good hand. The loud crack echoed throughout the cavern. Jerot's tear-filled eyes looked at Stella; she felt like she could have hit him again, "I deserved that," he whispered.

Jerot continued to wrap Stella's arm in silence. Every time he tightened the bandage, a bolt of pain went up Stella's arm and to her brain. By the time he was done, she had tears running down her face. "We should get you to one of the Healers. They have herbs and better bandages," Jerot said.

A great shadow appeared from the entrance of the nook. A large dragon of dark purple came into sight; it was Mullitor. "I heard a cry and thought I should investigate," he said. His eyes narrowed at what he saw: A shirtless Jerot kneeling over Stella, tears running down her cheeks and a bloody bandage covering her arm. "What's going on here?"

Jerot began to explain, but Stella cut him off, "I tripped and scraped my arm on that pink crystal," she said. "I wasn't watching where I was going."

"This crystal here?" Mullitor lowered his head and sniffed the blood that tipped the crystal.

"Yes," said Jerot. "It was an accident."

"Bad crystal," Mullitor scolded the crystal. "You should know better than to hurt my friends." Mullitor winked at Stella, which made her laugh.

Jerot reached for Stella's good arm, "Let's go see a Healer now."

Stella pulled back her arm. "I can get up on my own, thank you," she snapped.

Jerot led the way to the front of the cavern, followed by Stella and Mullitor.

"You are very lucky," Mullitor said to Stella. "The crystals here radiate a healing essence. Your injury should be healed in no time."

"That's amazing," said Stella.

"Yes, but having a Healer look at it wouldn't hurt," added Jerot. He weaved in and out of the campsites until he found a husband and wife with three children playing nearby. Jerot walked up to the woman; she was a small lady with long shocking red hair. "Behitha, we are in need of your services."

"Of course," Behitha smiled. "Were the goblins rough on you?"

"No," Jerot chuckled. "Stella fell and cut her arm,"

"Well, then, let's take a look," Behitha took Stella's arm and removed the bandage. "Looks deep, but I can fix it."

"I'll be back," said Jerot. "I need a new shirt and I'll fetch the Queen."

"Yeah, you do that," Stella seemed unimpressed with his words.

Behitha made a paste mixture of herbs and oils to apply onto Stella's arm. Stella expected it to sting like most healing agents, but instead it was cool and soothing. Behitha then wrapped Stella's arm with a proper bandage. "I should look at that again before bedtime."

"Okay," said Stella, "and thank you."

"Anytime, my dear."

Stella saw her grandmother coming towards her with Tuptup following behind. Her face was pale with fear. "I just got word from Jerot," said Queen Iona, "are you all right?"

"I think so," Stella rubbed her arm. "It was an accident."

"Okay," Queen Iona seemed relieved. "It seems those crystals can be dangerous," she turned to Mullitor, "no offense to your loved ones."

"None taken," Mullitor said.

"Come, it is almost time for lunch," Tuptup said. "I made some nice chicken soup."

"Sounds wonderful," said Stella.

"You will have to excuse me then," Mullitor said. "I am off to hunt for my own lunch," and he left the cavern through the tunnel out to the entrance.

The Queen had her own nook in the cavern, all set up with a tent and fancy pillows that served as chairs, surrounding a large fire pit. Tuptup poured three bowls of soup from a large cauldron sitting on a bed of hot coals. Stella expected Jerot to join them, but he was nowhere in sight. Stella supposed that was all right; she wasn't too happy with him anyway. The chicken soup was delicious and Stella ate a second bowl. The Queen finished her soup and leaned back in her pillow.

"So," said Queen Iona. "It was an accident?"

"Yes, why?"

"It just seems that Jerot looked guilty about the whole thing." Tuptup said while he enjoyed a second bowl of soup himself.

"Probably because he didn't move fast enough to catch me." Stella couldn't think of a better excuse.

The Queen and Tuptup looked at each other with doubtful looks, "I suppose that could be it," said Queen Iona. "I'd better fix that sweater for you," she added, pointing to Stella's sleeve. It was torn and starting to unravel.

Tuptup handed Stella a brown sweater to change into. "Is it fixable?" she asked.

"Oh yes," Queen Iona smiled. "I am a whiz at knitting."

After Mullitor returned, Stella spent the afternoon with him in a private niche of the cavern. The crystals glowed as they emitted their healing energy. She told him of all the wonderful things she did while in Las Vegas and they planned on their next flying adventure. Stella had long forgotten Jerot, who was still missing.

"I should show you Celadon Lake. It's south of the Welcome Garden and it is iced over by faint green ice. Very pretty." Mullitor said.

"That sounds wonderful." Stella.

"Once you are healed," Mullitor added, "we could also go to the city of Hansa. It's an entire city made of gold. You would love it."

Stella was going to reply when she was interrupted by the arrival of Jerot's squire, Dekel. He seemed flustered as he entered the small nook. "Sorry to barge in," he said, "but a messenger boy has come with a letter for you."

"From whom?" Stella wasn't expecting anything.

Dekel smiled widely. He said only one word. "Mistis."

"Mistis?" Mullitor seemed shocked. "Are you sure?"

"Who's Mistis?" Stella hated not knowing what's going on.

"Mistis is the grand oracle of Mayazure. She must see something in your future that is important enough to send you a letter."

Stella seemed skeptical. She didn't believe in fortune-telling, but perhaps the letter would humor her. "Take me to this messenger," she said to Dekel.

Dekel walked out to the tunnel, followed by Stella and Mullitor. Dekel took the lantern and led the way through the tunnel to the entrance of the cave.

The Queen was already there talking to the messenger. He was a young man in his early twenties with short orange hair. He was dressed in well-worn pants and a tunic; he looked more like a slave than a messenger.

"Ah, here is my granddaughter," Queen Iona said to the messenger as Stella arrived.

"I hear you have a letter for me," Stella said to the young man. He nodded and held out a small white envelope. Once Stella took it, the messenger bowed and left without saying a word. "Talkative, isn't he?" Stella said to Mullitor, who chuckled.

Stella ripped open the envelope and inside was a small piece of paper with fancy script handwriting. She had to look at it a few times to make out the words:

You are cordially invited to the Hall of Sight to speak to Mistis, the Grand Oracle of Mayazure, tomorrow. The Grand Oracle has had a vision that would most interest you.

"Odd" said Stella, "but I guess I can go. Wouldn't hurt."

"I can take you there," said Mullitor. "It's very far to the east and would take too long on horseback."

Stella smiled at the thought of riding Mullitor. "That would be great."

"Are you sure you should be riding with your injury?" Queen Iona asked with a slight concern.

"By tomorrow it will be healed," said Mullitor. "The soul crystals work fast."

Mullitor was correct. After a hearty dinner of pasta and vegetables, Stella went back to the Healer, Behitha, to check on her injury. Behitha unwrapped the bandage to reveal the injury was more like a cat scratch than a major wound.

"Well," said Behitha, "looks like you are healing nicely. Much better than I expected."

"Those crystals are really helping," added Stella.

Behitha applied more of the paste mixture on Stella's arm and placed a new bandage around it. "That should do until morning."

Stella thanked Behitha again for her services and made her way back to her grandmother, who was putting the finishing touches on Stella's sweater.

"There," said Queen Iona. "Good as new."

As Stella was putting her blue sweater back on, a thought crossed her mind: Jerot was still missing. Maybe she just didn't notice him somewhere else in the cavern; it was rather huge, after all, large enough to hide or get lost in. "You haven't seen Jerot, have you? He's been missing since lunch," Stella asked.

"I haven't," Queen Iona smiled, making Stella uncomfortable "Perhaps you should find him. He has yet to tell me about his trip to Wreckton."

Stella walked through the cavern to the rear. The farther she walked the fewer camps she passed. Soon she was away from the crowd, but she pressed on. She glanced into each little corner as she made her way to the far reaches. She was almost at the end when a small light in a nook caught her attention. It was a lonely campsite, with a small fire and a tiny blue tent, large enough for one person. If it weren't for the white heart with a gold crown painted on the side of the tent, Stella would have thought it was a stranger's, but the symbol gave away Jerot's location.

"Hello?" Stella said softly as she stepped up to the tent. "Are you in there?"

The flap of the tent flung open and Jerot poked his head out. At first he seemed happy to see Stella, but then his smile faded. "I didn't want you to find me."

"Well, my grandmother is looking for you."

"Liar."

"Well, I certainly don't want to talk to you," this was a lie. Stella was glad to see Jerot was at least all right.

Jerot crawled out of the tent, wearing a new tunic. "Is your arm okay?" He went to reach for it, but Stella pulled back.

"It's fine. I hope I didn't ruin your best shirt."

"I don't have emotional attachment to material things," Jerot seemed agitated. "It wasn't my best shirt anyway," he tried to smile, but Stella was still annoyed. The memories of this morning were starting to come back to her. "I am truly sorry," Jerot said. "I would never mean to hurt you."

"Well, you did," Stella snapped. "Now come on. My grandmother is waiting." Stella walked to the front of the cavern. She wasn't sure Jerot was following her; she didn't bother to look over her shoulder. Jerot followed in silence and didn't speak until they reached the corner of the cavern where the Queen camped.

"I apologize for my absence," said Jerot. "I had some personal matters to deal with."

"It's quite alright," Queen Iona smiled. "What have you learned from the goblins?"

"Wreckton wants to remain neutral, I'm afraid, but they are happy to sell us anything we need to survive."

Tuptup snorted, "Anything to make money."

"Well, that is better than nothing," Queen Iona smiled. "Why don't you go back tomorrow and buy more supplies. I believe we are low on food."

"You can come with me," Jerot turned to Stella. "You would like Wreckton."

"I can't," Stella said hastily. "I am going with Mullitor to see Mistis."

"Mistis?" Jerot was shocked. "Why would she want to see you?"

"It's none of your business."

"It seems she has seen a vision that is important enough to share with Stella." Queen Iona said.

"If you were around earlier, you would have known that," Stella added.

Jerot frowned, "Well it's too bad you can't go to Wreckton. Maybe next time."

"Doubt it."

Jerot excused himself to go back to his camp, leaving Stella with her grandmother and Tuptup.

"Why are you so angry with him?" asked Queen Iona.

"It's his fault I hurt myself."

"I thought it was an accident."

"It was," Stella said, "but I wouldn't have tripped if he wasn't there to distract me."

"You shouldn't be so hard on him," Tuptup said. "He is a sensitive creature."

"And stupid," Stella muttered.

"No matter," said Queen Iona. "It is late and almost time for bed." Stella saw parents calling their children to come inside the tents for bed. Mullitor had found a nesting spot of his own and was curled up like a large dog just entering the twilight of sleep. "You can sleep in my tent with Tuptup and me," said Queen Iona.

Stella entered the large blue tent. She changed into a pink nightgown and settled onto one of three large cots while her grandmother and Tuptup did the same. Three Minots were also preparing for sleep, nestling in a pile of old cloths. Stella laid staring at the ceiling of the tent. An hour passed and she still was awake. Perhaps a walk would help her sleep.

Stella left the tent and walked through the campsites. Most people were asleep. A few were still awake, enjoying a late night smoke of their pipes or a sip of tea. Stella made her way to the sleeping dragon, who was snoring peacefully. She gently touched Mullitor and woke him up.

"Can't sleep?"

"No," Stella answered. "I have too much on my mind."

"I understand," said Mullitor. "You have witnessed many things today. How is your arm?"

"It feels fine," Stella sat down next to Mullitor and leaned up against his side. The soft fleece-like skin was warm and inviting. "I'm a little nervous about seeing Mistis. I wonder what she saw."

"Well, we will find out tomorrow, won't we?"

"I just hope it is something good. I need some good news."

"We could all use some good news," Mullitor answered. Stella nodded in agreement.

Mullitor closed his eyes and soon fell asleep again. Stella watched the faintly glowing crystals and could feel herself slowly falling into a slumber. She watched a reflection of herself in a large yellow crystal. A flash of the mysterious women also appeared, but Stella was too tired to care. Mullitor's gentle snoring eased Stella and she could barely keep her eyes open. Soon she was fast asleep and all was darkness.

The Tree

The first thing Stella did when she awoke was look at her left arm. There, a small scratch was all that remained of her injury. It was hardly noticeable. "That's good enough proof that I haven't been crazy for months," she said to Roxanne, who was sitting at the foot of the bed, waiting for breakfast.

Stella got out of bed, put her grandmother's ring in her silver jewelry box, put on her glasses and tiptoed past the bathroom, where Ryan was taking his morning shower. She walked down to the kitchen and fed the cat before getting herself a bowl of cereal. She thought of all the things she had to do today: Go to her office to grade the students' final projects, clean the house in preparation for Christmas dinner in a few days and wrap presents. Yes, she was going to be a busy bee.

Ryan joined Stella in the kitchen where a bowl of cereal was waiting for him. He seemed less cheery than usual and grunted as he ate. "Do I have to go to work?" he muttered.

"Yes, vacation is over," Stella rubbed his shoulders and kissed his ear. "I don't want to do stuff either, but that's life."

Again Ryan grunted. "Life sucks." Stella giggled.

Once Ryan left and Stella took her shower, she grabbed her purse and sketchbook and went outside. The ground was still covered in snow, but driving wasn't as bad, now that all the college students were gone. Stella parked behind the art building, as usual and walked in through the back door. Even though she wasn't on a rigid schedule, Stella still looked at the clock to check the time: it was a little before 9 o'clock.

Stella went upstairs towards her office, but she stopped at the art gallery's glass wall. She stared at the glass, remembering the image of that strange blonde woman from a couple weeks earlier. Today, there was nothing but Stella's own reflection.

Stella went to her classroom. All the desks were still in their neat rows. Each one had a sculpture set on it. Stella set her things down on her desk and got to work looking at the sculptures. There were twenty-two of them to grade. They would be judged on how well the sculpture looked, as well as how well the emotion was expressed. Stella didn't take grading lightly. She was tough, but fair.

Stella opened her sketchbook; she would make notes on each piece as she graded. The first sculpture was a ceramic piece of a little girl crying over a dropped ice cream cone. Stella wrote down the student's name on her sketchbook and then studied the sculpture from different angles. There was some sloppiness around the base and she noted it in her sketchbook. She read the essay that went with it: a short story about a little girl's first ice cream cone and her bad experience. Not a very creative story, but the emotion was clearly there in the sculpture. Stella put a large B in her sketchbook and moved to the next sculpture.

Three hours later, Stella finished grading all the projects. Stella looked over her sketchbook: eight As, ten Bs and four Cs. "Looks like everyone's going to pass," Stella said to herself. She put the sketchbook down and began moving the sculptures to her office. Though it was a small room, there was space enough for the sculptures on the floor. Once everything was moved to the office, Stella sat at her desk and turned on her computer. She opened the grading program and began to insert students' names and their final grades into the system. In fifteen minutes, she had completely entered all the information. Stella smiled; she was finally done with the semester.

Stella locked her office and went outside to her car. It was now well past noon and she was getting hungry.

Stella decided to treat herself to a burger from her favorite fast food place. Sure, it's bad for you, she told herself, but Stella knew she would work off those calories while cleaning. As she sat at a booth eating, she flipped through her sketchbook and doodled a little. Art never takes a break, even for lunch.

Stella opened the front door of her house and was greeted by Roxanne. She weaved in between Stella's legs and purred while Stella put some cat food in a dish for her. "I'm going to clean, so don't be a pest, okay?" Stella pet the cat while she ate.

Stella was hosting Christmas this year, so the house had to be immaculate or as close to it as possible. Stella grabbed a cloth and got to work dusting all the tables and knick-knacks. Dusting was such a chore; having to move everything and wipe it all down. She hummed a tune while she cleaned picture frames and dusted the coffee table in the living room.

Stella then got to work cleaning the two bathrooms, scrubbing the bathtubs and the toilets as well as sweeping the tile floors, followed by a good mopping. She collected all the towels and threw them in the washing machine. By late afternoon, Stella was running the vacuum around the house. Roxanne watched the roaring beast from a safe distance. Stella moved the couch and all the furniture to sweep behind and underneath. By the time all the sweeping was done it was 4 o'clock and Stella was exhausted.

"Well, what do you think?" she asked the cat as she put the vacuum away. Roxanne simply meowed. "Now let's try and keep it clean until after Christmas."

After putting the towels in the dryer, Stella made her way upstairs to the spare bedroom, which was a temporary storage place for all the Christmas presents. She wrapped the gifts including her gift to Ryan (Stella had bought him a few music CDs he wanted and a new watch, which he needed). She laid out the giftwrap and carefully wrapped the purse she got for Aunt Shelly, folding the paper and taping it down with precision. She cut some ribbon and fashioned a bow on top. Roxanne watched Stella work and pounced on a piece of runaway ribbon. Stella giggled and dragged the ribbon across the floor for the cat, who chased it. While Stella wrapped her dad's gift, Roxanne discovered an empty box to hide in. She looked over the side of the box at Stella and when the right opportunity struck, she would pop out and attack any intriguing piece of paper or ribbon.

Once Stella was done with all the wrapping, she moved the gifts downstairs in the living room next to where the Christmas tree would be erected. They used an artificial tree, because Stella didn't like the idea of cutting down a beautiful tree to only be thrown away.

Stella went down to the basement and pulled out the large box where the tree was stored, as well as all the decorations and lights. She managed to get everything to the living room when Ryan came home from work.

"You are just in time to help me with the tree," Stella kissed her husband. "You can put the tree together while I make dinner."

"Sounds like a plan. Let me go change out of this suit." Ryan went upstairs while Stella removed the towels from the dryer and put them away before digging through the pantry to decide on what to make for dinner.

A few minutes later, Stella was cooking macaroni and cheese and cutting up vegetables for a salad while Ryan set up the tree. Every minute or so, she would hear him curse as he struggled to put the parts in the right place. Stella couldn't help but chuckle to herself. She set the table and dished out all the food before checking on Ryan, who had completed half the tree.

"Come take a break and eat," she said. "I'll help you after dinner."

Ryan told Stella about his day at the insurance company where he worked. "I had meetings all day," he said. "I wanted to work on some pending claims, but I never had a chance. I am so far behind. Tomorrow is going to be a busy day for me."

"I think I'll do the rest of the decorating tomorrow," Stella said. "Let's just finish the tree tonight. You look tired already."

"But I like decorating."

"I can do it. I'm a big girl," Stella smiled. "You need to save your energy for work. My work is done, so I'll take care of all the decorating."

Stella did the dishes while Ryan put the rest of the tree together. She joined him just in time to string the lights. After carefully putting on the lights, Stella wrapped the tree in gold garland. Roxanne kept pouncing on the garland pile as it moved. "Bad kitty!" Ryan shooed her away where she took refuge behind the couch.

Once the garland was in place, Ryan opened the box of ornaments. There where all shapes and sizes, all in shades of red. Some were the typical balls while others were long icicles or geometrical shapes. Stella started with a red heart-shaped ornament and began putting the rest on the tree. The trick was to not have the same shapes next to each other. Ryan grabbed a few of the brightly red balls and spaced them out on the tree. Soon there were stars, diamonds, birds, snowflakes and even cube-shaped ornaments on the tree.

When the final red ornament was placed, Stella opened a smaller box that stored the gold star topper and handed it to Ryan. He was taller and could reach the very top of the tree.

"Well," Ryan said plugging in the lights, "What do you think?

Stella took a step back and looked at the tree. The white lights illuminated the gold and red spectacularly. "It looks beautiful," she said.

"I think it's the best tree in town," Ryan winked at Stella and she giggled.

"Help me put these boxes away and then you can chill out for the rest of the evening." Stella picked up a few

of the boxes and went down to the
basement with Ryan. Once everything
was back in order, they took refuge on
the couch and watched the evening
news.

Stella listened to the television
while she dabbled in her sketchbook.
She flipped through the pages and
found the drawing of the unknown
blonde woman. She still didn't know
who she was or why she had been
seeing her. Stella flipped to a doodle
that she had started at lunchtime and
continued it. It was a forest landscape
much like in Mayazure. She drew a
deer with her fawn grazing on the
grass while a full moon shown in the
sky. By the time she finished her
drawing, it was late in the evening and
Roxanne was begging for food. The
cat meowed loudly and clawed at
Stella's pant leg.

"Okay, okay," Stella put down the
sketchbook and followed the cat to
the kitchen where she opened a can of
cat food and put it on a plate. Once
the hungry beast was fed, Stella went
back to the living room where Ryan

was looking at Stella's newest drawing. "Oh don't look at that. It's just a doodle."

"It's not that bad," Ryan smiled. "Next time, draw something more unusual, like aliens or something."

Stella kissed her husband, "I think I'm going to go to bed."

"I'll be up in a little bit," Ryan said as Stella walked over to the glimmering Christmas tree and turned off the lights before heading upstairs.

Stella looked at her arm and saw that is was almost completely healed. She changed into a warmer nightgown and opened her jewelry box to see her grandmother's ring waiting for her. She slipped it on and removed her glasses before crawling into bed. She stared at the ceiling thinking about her invitation to see Mistis. She wondered what the oracle could have seen that had to be shared. Stella's eyes grew heavier as she laid in bed. The blowing winter wind howled faintly outside, bellowing a chilling lullaby. Before Ryan joined her, Stella was fast asleep.

The Oracle

Just like the day before, Jerot was not waiting for Stella at the Welcome Garden, which was a slight disappointment. Instead, Jerot's apprentice, Dekel, was hiding amongst the flowers. "Good morning," he said handing Stella a cloak. "Sir Catosan couldn't be here, for he is getting ready to go to Wreckton," he said, as if he knew what Stella was wondering.

"Whatever," Stella said. She was still a little angry with him.

"Let us make haste then. Behitha wants to see you before you go to visit the oracle."

"Oh," Stella said, "but my arm is fine. See?" she rolled up the sleeve of her sweater to show Dekel her arm. There was no sign of any cut to be seen now.

"She still would like to see you. She will be happy that you are okay," Dekel smiled and led the way out of the garden.

They walked cautiously to the fork in the road. Stella couldn't help but look to the right where Sinopia use to be. She wondered what it looked like, whether the buildings were destroyed or not. Instead of going left or right at the fork, Dekel went straight ahead into the forest, followed closely by Stella.

They walked north, the thick snow crunching beneath their feet, until they arrived at Bondi Field. From there, they took the small path to the Cave of Eternal Blaze. Once inside, her grandmother and Tuptup greeted Stella.

"How is your arm?" Queen Iona asked with concern.

Stella showed her the now fully healed spot of her arm. "All better."

"I knew the crystals would heal you well," said a deep voice. It was Mullitor, who had come from the back of the cavern to join them.

"Care for some breakfast?" Tuptup asked. "I'm afraid all I can make is eggs."

"That would be fine," Stella said.

"We should leave shortly anyway," Mullitor added,. "The trip east to Mistis will be long."

While Tuptup prepared breakfast, Stella went looking for Behitha at her campsite. Stella showed the Healer her arm. "Well, it looks like you are all better," Behitha said. "My work here is done."

"Thank you for your services," Stella said.

"Anytime my dear, anytime," Behitha smiled.

Stella made her way back to her grandmother's campsite, where scrambled eggs and toast awaited her. After a quick meal, Stella said goodbye to her grandmother and left with Mullitor.

"Be careful," Queen Iona said, "and tell Mistis I said hello."

"She's an oracle," Stella said. "She'll already know." Tuptup and Mullitor laughed at Stella's joke.

"So true, but tell her anyway."

Stella followed Mullitor through the tunnel and to the entrance of the cave. She climbed up onto his back and he took off into the air.

"Do you think we could make a quick pass over Sinopia?" Stella asked. "I want to see what it looks like."

"I think I could do that," Mullitor said, "but there isn't much left. The trolls have all but destroyed it. For some reason, they like to live in ruins."

Mullitor went slightly southward towards Sinopia. He stayed high above, so the trolls couldn't shoot at him with arrows. Stella looked down. The castle was all but destroyed; only large boulders and rocks were left. Very few buildings were still standing, and those were overgrown with weeds; the walls and roofs had holes in them. Brick walkways were now reduced to broken paths, much like the path at the fork in the road from the Welcome Garden.

"What a mess," said Stella.

"Indeed," Mullitor said. "They are not very good housekeepers."

Mullitor swung up and headed northeast until he flew to Chamoisee Canyon and then traveled east. The canyon was dusted with a fine layer of snow, but the rust color could still be seen peeking out from under the snow. Once past the canyon, Mullitor continued east over the vast forest of leaf-less trees. For an hour, all Stella saw was the forest, an occasional hill or small pool of frozen water, but mostly just snow-covered trees covered the land.

Stella was becoming bored when she spotted a large lake up ahead that was not quite frozen yet.

"What's that?" she asked Mullitor.

"That is Seer Lake," Mullitor said. "It is where Mistis lives." He landed gently at the shore of the lake, near a bridge. "You go across the bridge until it ends. There you will find Mistis."

Stella slipped off of Mullitor's back and mounted the bridge. "I'll try not to be long," she said.

"Take your time," Mullitor smiled back.

The bridge was sturdy and made of heavy wood, but was only wide enough for a single person to cross it. Stella held onto the rails as she walked. *Does this bridge go across the whole lake?* she thought. That would be a long journey. *Maybe it goes to an island.*

Stella walked for at least a half a mile before she saw that the bridge ended at a door in the middle of the lake. It was just a door; no building or house was attached. As Stella came closer, she saw she was not alone on the bridge. Sitting by the door was an orange cat. He was well fed and had a huge nose, as if it was stung by a bee and swollen permanently.

"Hello there, little kitty," Stella said once she reached the door. "You are a cute little guy, aren't you?"

"Hello yourself," answered the cat to Stella's surprise. "You must be Stella Tyrian. Mistis has been waiting for you."

"Oh sorry. I didn't realize you could talk. Yes, I'm Stella Tyrian."

"Of course I can talk," the cat seemed agitated.

"It's just that where I come from, animals don't talk," Stella felt ashamed. "Again, I'm sorry."

"Quite alright. Now let's go inside," the cat pawed at the door.

"Inside?" Stella leaned to look past the door. The rest of the lake was on the other side, "Won't we just end up in the lake?"

The cat looked at Stella and seemed to smile. "Looks can be deceiving." He gave the door a final push and it opened revealing a room of white. "Come on," the cat said.

Stella stepped over the threshold and entered into a vast room so big, she didn't see any walls. She looked behind her to see the bridge and the lake through the door, but around the door was a white room. The cat pushed the door shut and the lake, the bridge and even Mullitor were gone from view.

"This way," the cat walked straight away, followed by Stella. The floor of the room was pristine and large white columns held up the white ceiling. Every once in a while, Stella looked back to see the door getting smaller and smaller and finally disappearing from view. After walking for a bit, Stella struck up a conversation.

"What is this place?"

"It is the Hall of Sight," the cat answered.

"How big is it?"

"It goes on forever. You have to know where you're going or you'll be lost."

"Have you ever gotten lost?" Stella asked.

"Not yet." The cat continued walking straight.

"I didn't get your name. Do you have one?"

The cat stopped and grinned. "I am Radam. Guardian of Mistis."

"You're her guardian?" Stella found this humorous, as Radam seemed too small to guard anything but a bowl of food.

"Yes. I may be small, but I am tough."

Radam continued straight ahead and Stella followed. Soon, she saw a figure. As they got closer, Stella was able to make out a large pile of pillows in multiple bright colors. In the center of the pile sat a plump woman. She was robed in gold satin and her hair fell in blonde curls. She was sitting in a lotus position, meditating peacefully.

"Hate to disturb you," Radam said to the woman. "but Stella Tyrian is here."

The woman opened her eyes. They were a mixture of blue and green. "I already knew that," she said.

"You must be Mistis," Stella made a slight bow. "It is a pleasure to meet you."

"As is a pleasure to meet you," Mistis turned to Radam. "Why don't you go find the kitchen area and have some lunch brought to us?"

Radam nodded and trotted away. Both Stella and Mistis watched him go until he disappeared.

Mistis slipped off her pillows. She was short and just as round. She looked like a golden ball instead of a woman. "Why don't we go find a suitable place to sit and have lunch?" Mistis walked down the same path as Radam, leading Stella with her.

They walked a few hundred feet down the hall until they reached a short white table; two large red pillows where placed on either end. Mistis sat down on one while Stella took her place on the other.

"So, you had a vision about me?" Stella asked.

"Yes," Mistis shifted her robes, "but we will talk about that after lunch. How do you like Mayazure so far?"

"I love it here, but I bet you knew that already."

Mistis giggled, "Yes, yes I did."

From Stella's right, a young man approached. It was the messenger who had brought the message to Stella the day before. He was still dressed in the worn pants and tunic, and was now holding a tray full of food and a tea set. He put the tray down on the table without saying a word.

"Thank you dear," Mistis smiled. The young man nodded and left.

"Are there lots of people in here?" Stella asked.

"I have several servants," Mistis said while pouring tea into two cups. "I don't see some of them for days, but I love them all like my children. Now, let's see what we have here."

The tray was loaded with different types of bread and three bowls of spread. One was definitely butter while the other two were foreign to Stella. One looked like cream cheese with specks of yellow in it and the other was a deep red jam.

"What are those?" Stella asked.

Mistis pointed to the one with the yellow specks. "Oh, that one is a cheese spread with crushed Lolly. That is a herb. The other is gelled Mukluk blood."

"Mukluk?"

"Yes, a type of fish. It is very sweet. Try it."

Stella took a slice of wheat bread and dipped her butter knife into the gelled blood. She spread just the corner of her bread and took a bite. She expected it to taste awful, but Mistis was right; it was sweet like strawberry jelly. Stella tried the cheese spread with Lolly. The herb had a garlic-like taste to it.

"How is it?" asked Mistis.

"Pretty good."

"I'm glad. I'm not too fond of the Lolly, but I had a feeling you would like it," Mistis winked, making Stella laugh.

"Is there anything you don't already know?" Stella tried the butter spread on a piece of rye bread.

Mistis smiled as she spread some of the Mukluk blood on a piece of pita bread. They ate in silence. Stella tasted all the types of bread and soon was full. Radam returned, "Is there anything else that you need?" the cat asked Mistis.

"Perhaps," Mistis took a sip of her tea. "Stella, I am now ready to tell you of my vision."

Stella became nervous, "Okay."

"As you know, the former princess of Sinopia has taken over Cobalian."

"Yes. Stella Cinereous."

Mistis leaned forward as if she was about to divulge a secret, as if others were around to hear. "You must not, under any circumstance, fight her alone."

"Is that it?" Stella seemed disappointed.

"No," Mistis patted Radam on the head. "I am releasing Radam of his guardian duties. From now on he will be your guardian until it is safe for you to be alone."

"But you will be vulnerable," Radam said to Mistis.

"In the many years I have been alive, no one has attacked here. I am sure I will be fine."

"That is because no one dared to challenge me. Surely you must reconsider."

"I have seen the future and I know I am safe," Mistis smiled. "Now you two must head back. It will be late by the time your dragon friend takes you back to the Cave of Eternal Blaze."

Stella stood up. "It was a pleasure meeting you. Thanks for lunch. It was very good."

Mistis rose from her pillow as well. She walked over to Stella and took her hand. "The pleasure is all mine. There is one more thing I must tell you."

"What is that?"

"Forgive your friend, Jerot. He is suffering, because you still feel ill will towards him. He never meant to hurt you."

"I was going to forgive him anyway," Stella said, offended.

"Good," Mistis smiled. "The sooner, the better. Farewell then."

Radam led the way back to the portal door. Stella opened the door to reveal the bridge and the lake. They crossed over and Stella closed the door to the Hall of Sight. As they walked across the bridge, Radam muttered to himself.

"I am not so sure about leaving Mistis alone."

"But she's not really alone," Stella said. "She does have other servants."

"Oh yes, but they are not skilled at protecting her."

"She said she would be fine. You must trust her."

"I do trust her," Radam said, "but I don't believe her."

Mullitor was waiting for them as they reached the end of the bridge, "Who is this little creature?" he asked Stella.

"Mullitor, this is Radam," Stella introduced the cat. "He is Mistis' guardian. He will be joining us on the trip back. Mistis said I need him more than she does."

Mullitor looked down at the orange cat. "Tell me, Radam, have you ever flown before?"

"I haven't," Radam pawed the ground nervously. "Please be gentle."

"I always am."

Stella scooped up the cat in her arms and climbed onto Mullitor's back. Radam dug his claws into Stella's sweater as further precaution. Mullitor took off and his flying was indeed more gentle than usual. He flew slowly over Mayazure. Radam looked down to see the snow-covered land. A massive river was no more than a thin line and hills were but small bumps dotting the ground.

"Oh my," he said, "perhaps I shouldn't look down."

"You will get use to it," said Stella.

"I will go lower if that pleases you," Mullitor added.

"I think that would be a good idea," Radam shivered.

Mullitor flew lower, only a few feet above the treetops. Stella held onto Radam tightly, and soon he no longer shivered in fear. After an hour of slow flying, Radam became brave enough to look down again, starting to enjoy his flight.

"I hardly go beyond Seer Lake," he said. "All of this is new to me."

"You have never seen the rest of Mayazure?" Stella asked.

"No, I was born in the Hall of Sight and I planned on just staying there."

"Sounds awfully boring to me," Mullitor chimed in. "I would surely go mad if I never left my cave."

"You are different," said Stella. "You were meant to go long distances, but Radam is so tiny." She turned her attention to Radam. "The Hall of Sight is endless. I bet you have traveled more than you know."

"This is true," the orange cat looked down again. "Can you tell me what we are flying over?"

Stella pointed out to Radam specific areas as they flew over them (Mullitor filled in any details that Stella didn't know). They soon were over Chamoisee Canyon and past Bondi Field. By the time they reached the Cave of Eternal Blaze, the sun was low in the horizon and the sky was a deep blue. Long shadows marked the ground and only the brightest stars shown in the sky.

Mullitor landed at the cave entrance and Stella dismounted before placing Radam on the ground. He purred happily and kneaded the floor of the cave, feeling the dirt between his toes.

"That was a wonderful ride," he said, "but I am glad to be back on the ground. What is this place called?"

"This is the Cave of Eternal Blaze," said Mullitor. "It is also my home." Mullitor led Stella and Radam through the tunnel and into the cavern. Radam was in awe of its beauty and saddened that so many civilian refugees now lived inside among the crystals.

"Come," Stella said. "You have to meet my grandma. She is the Queen of Cobalian." She led the way to the Queen's campsite and introduced Radam to her grandmother and Tuptup.

"It is a pleasure to meet you, Radam," Queen Iona said as she patted the orange cat.

"He is Mistis' guardian," Stella explained. "He was assigned by Mistis to protect me."

"A guardian?" Tuptup seemed unimpressed. "Mistis having mouse troubles?" he laughed at his own joke.

"I assure you I am very skilled at protection," Radam's ears laid flat on his head, clearly offended.

"I'm sure you are a great guardian," Queen Iona added. "Mistis must see a great future for you, if she wants you to watch over my granddaughter."

"Yeah," said Tuptup. "What did Mistis see anyway?"

Stella told them what Mistis said, that she was not to battle Stella the Subjugator alone and Radam's duty was to guard her.

"Of course you would never fight alone," Tuptup snorted. "This is a battle over a city, not over a boy. Such foolishness."

Radam was losing his patience with the dwarf. "How dare you call my mistress foolish! She is a respected seer and her visions are never wrong."

"Oh no," Tuptup bowed low. "I would never call Mistis a fool. Forgive me." Radam reluctantly forgave Tuptup, but it was clear the cat didn't trust him.

"Perhaps dinner will help us all relax," Queen Iona smiled. "I'm hungry and I'm sure everyone else is." Dinner was pleasant. The bread and fancy spreads Stella had eaten long ago were no longer keeping her appetite at bay. Everyone ate peacefully, but Jerot's absence was noticed. Before Stella could ask, Mullitor spoke what she was thinking.

"I see no Jerot here. Has he returned from Wreckton?"

"Aye," Tuptup answered. "But his trip was tiring and he retired to his campsite."

"Who's Jerot?" Radam's curiosity was piqued.

"He is my best knight," Queen Iona beamed.

"Didn't Mistis mention him?" Radam turned to Stella. "Something about forgiving him?"

"Did she?" Queen Iona grinned slightly.

"Well, yes she did," Stella felt her cheeks getting warm. "I suppose I should go talk to him." She arose.

"I will go with you," Radam too stood up.

"I think Stella will be okay without you for a few moments," Queen Iona said. "Besides, I would like to know about Mistis and how she's doing. You have to tell me."

"Well…" Radam thought for a moment, "I guess we're all safe here."

Stella bid farewell and wandered through the campsites until she spotted Jerot's in the back. The flaps of his tent were open and Jerot was sitting by a small fire, cooking sausages over the flames. At the sight of Stella approaching, he stood.

"You're back." He gave an awkward smile. "How was your visit to the oracle?"

"It was fine," Stella said, and then explained what Mistis had seen.

"How odd," Jerot sat back down and continued to roast his sausage. Stella squatted down a few feet from him. "Care for a sausage?"

"No thanks. I just ate."

"I wonder what Mistis meant. I guess it means no dueling."

"But I don't even know Stella Cinereous and she doesn't know who I am."

"At least not yet," Jerot twirled his sausage around in the fire. "When we do battle, you'll get to know her plenty."

An awkward silence followed. Stella watched the fire as it danced around Jerot's sausage. "I wanted to say that I forgive you for yesterday," Stella voice was soft. "I know you didn't mean it."

Jerot propped the skewer that held his sausage against a crystal, reached over and wrapped Stella in a massive hug, her face buried in his chest. "Thank you, thank you," he repeated over and over again. He finally let her go and Stella could see he was smiling broadly. "How is your arm anyway?"

Stella rolled up the sleeve of her sweater to reveal her healed arm, "All better," she smiled. "The crystals and the work of Behitha made it heal very well."

"I am glad. I would never have forgiven myself, if you were scarred."

Jerot finished cooking his sausage while Stella told him about the Hall of Sight and of Radam. Jerot had never seen where Mistis lived and Stella told him in great detail of Seer Lake and the bridge to the door in the middle of nowhere that opened to a never-ending room with columns. She described Mistis, the short round woman in gold robes and fancy pillows. Stella enlightened him on the Lolly spread and the spread made of Mukluk blood.

"Sounds like a better adventure than mine," Jerot chewed his food.

"How was Wreckton?"

"It was quite dull. I gathered up a few of the other knights and we went by horseback to get there. Since they don't go as fast as Mullitor, the trip was a long and boring one."

"Maybe next time I could go with you," Stella said.

"Yes, I was planning on going again after Christmas. I would love to bring you along," Jerot placed another sausage on the skewer. "You would love it there. The Goblins are an advanced people. They have a lot of great things there."

"Sounds like a plan."

Stella spent the rest of the evening with Jerot. After he was full, he went into his tent and bought out a small guitar. He strummed cords and hummed softly. "I'm afraid I don't know any good songs," he said.

"That's okay. You play very well." Stella was a sucker for musicians.

Jerot continued to play, his hands gliding over the strings, his humming soothing to Stella's ear. Soon she was feeling sleepy and was yawning.

"It looks like you might be tired," Jerot stopped playing. "You had a long day."

"You're right, "Stella yawned again. "I guess I will go now and get some sleep." They both got to their feet and again, Jerot hugged her.

"Maybe tomorrow you can help me write a song," he said.

"That would be fun. We could practice more archery tomorrow too."

"I would like that."

Stella said goodbye and walked back to the front of the cavern. Many of the villagers were packing up for the night and Mullitor was already nestled in among the crystals. She stopped by to wish him good night.

"Pleasant dreams," Stella patted his head and he purred softly.

"You won't be joining me tonight?" Mullitor seemed disappointed.

"I think I will be able to sleep fine tonight in grandma's tent."

"Very well," Mullitor laid his head down between his two front feet. "Have a peaceful sleep."

Stella arrived at her grandmother's tent, where the Queen was already dressed for the night and was sitting on a small pillow, sipping on a cup of tea. Tuptup was laying on one of the cots, his hands folded behind his head while he stared at the ceiling of the tent. Radam had made a nest with the Minots and was already asleep for the night.

"Back so soon?" Queen Iona asked.

"It's getting late and I am tired," Stella slipped out of her sweater and jeans and put on her pink nightgown.

"At least come and have a cup of tea with me."

Stella sat down on a small pillow while the Queen poured a second cup of tea. The steam tickled her nose and the scent of peppermint rose faintly in the air. Stella sipped the tea and savored the mint taste.

"I am very glad you forgave Jerot," Queen Iona said, "Now I won't have a moody knight to deal with."

Stella chuckled, "I was going to forgive him anyway. I'm not one to hold grudges forever."

"Very true, plus Christmas is only a few days away. You don't want to be angry on Christmas."

"That reminds me," Stella added, "I have to finish decorating the house. Christmas will be at our house this year."

"How lovely. I do miss my daughters, as well as Ferdinand and Dominic."

"I'll give Mom and Aunt Shelly an extra hug from you."

"That would be nice," Queen Iona took a sip of tea.

Stella finished her tea and gave her grandmother a kiss on the cheek, "Goodnight Grandma."

"Good night, dear," Queen Iona smiled.

Stella took one of the empty cots and settled in for the night. She watched Radam's slow rhythmic breathing and soon she was fast asleep.

The Santas

Stella's alarm blared its annoying tune and she rolled over and hit the snooze button. After it went off the second time, she turned it off and sat up. She rubbed her eyes and took in the morning sunlight that shone through the window. How deceiving the sun was, since she knew it was freezing outside and the ground was covered in snow. Stella hesitantly pulled herself out of bed and put away her grandmother's ring. Roxanne weaved around Stella's legs while Stella cleaned her glasses on the hem of her nightshirt and put them on. She walked past the bathroom were Ryan was singing in the shower, performing his own private concert.

Stella stumbled sleepily down the stairs and entered the kitchen were she fed the cat before deciding on breakfast. She cracked a few eggs and scrambled them in a skillet, while bacon cooked in another. The fragrant smells filled the kitchen. By the time Ryan came down, breakfast was done and Stella was more awake.

"Mmm, bacon," Ryan inhaled deeply, "smells good."

They took their place at the dining room table. Stella poked at her eggs and nibbled her bacon while Ryan quickly devoured his meal. Stella couldn't help but think of what Mistis said. Why would the oracle tell her not to fight Stella the Subjugator alone, when no one expected her to?

"Not hungry?" Ryan asked between bites of egg.

"It's still too hot for me," Stella lied. She picked up a piece of bacon and ate it just to make her husband happy.

After breakfast, Stella kissed Ryan goodbye. "When you come home, everything will be ready for Christmas."

"I love how you decorate."

"Don't forget to wrap my presents… if you've bought them already," Stella teased.

"Maybe I did and maybe I didn't," Ryan winked, making Stella laugh.

With Ryan gone, Stella washed the dishes and headed to the shower. She turned the water on extra warm for she was colder than usual. The hot water felt good and she hopped out of the shower and dressed in jeans and a heavy sweatshirt.

Stella went to the basement to find the rest of the Christmas decorations. She walked past her sculpting area to the corner. The first box was loaded with lights of multiple colors. Stella untangled them and plugged in each set to make sure they worked. After passing inspection, Stella carefully lined each window of the house with lights. Roxanne helped by playing with the lights as Stella dragged them around. She then took the longest string of lights and draped them along the front porch. Since the house was so tall, this was the only lights she put up outdoors.

Stella pulled out a long piece of evergreen garland and two stockings, one red and one gold. She wrapped the garland around the staircase. The house didn't have a fireplace, so Stella simply tacked the two stockings to the lower steps of the staircase. She grabbed the watch she bought for Ryan and placed it inside the gold stocking.

By the time she was done putting up the lights and the stockings, it was lunchtime. Stella made herself a sandwich with bologna and cheese topped with mayonnaise and ketchup, and a glass of soda. She was going to need the caffeine to keep her awake, so she could finish decorating.

Stella headed back down to the basement once more and opened another box. Inside was a large collection of Santas, at least thirty of them. Stella dragged the box upstairs and began to place the Santas around the house; on the bookshelf in the upstairs hallway, on the end tables in the living room and even on the television stand. A snow globe with a cheery Santa inside went on the coffee table. There were skinny Santas, fat Santas, some made of wax, others made of wood and a few made of ceramic. At the bottom of the box was a large Santa nutcracker. This, Stella put by the front door, as if his job was to greet visitors.

Stella finally found the last Christmas decoration, the wreath for the front door. It was a massive wreath decorated with small red and gold berries and a large red bow. It had become slightly misshapen, so Stella fluffed out the greenery as best she could. She opened the front door and carefully placed the wreath on the small hook in the middle of the door. She stood back to admire the wreath before shutting the front door. Stella was finally done with the decorating and decided on a cup of tea.

She filled the teakettle that had once belonged to her grandmother and placed it on the stove. While the water boiled, Stella reached up in the cupboard and chose a green tea, placing the tea bag in a mug as well as a few spoonfuls of sugar. Soon the water boiled and Stella poured the hot steaming water into the mug and let the tea steep for a few minutes.

Stella took her mug and sat herself on the couch in the living room. Roxanne joined her and laid down next to her. She sipped the tea as she gently rubbed the cat. She couldn't help but think of meeting Radam. Stella reached over to the coffee table and grabbed the Santa snow globe. She tipped it upside down and then upright again, watching the fake snow swirl inside, her face reflected in the glass. The happy Santa inside made Stella smile. Again she flipped the snow globe around and watched the snow spin about.

In a flash, the mysterious blonde woman appeared next to Stella's reflection, almost causing Stella to drop the snow globe. She swore and looked into the glass again, but all she saw was her frightened face looking back. Stella put the snow globe down on the coffee table and shook her head.

"I need to stop looking at myself," Stella finished her tea. "Am I crazy?" she asked Roxanne, who was unfazed by what had just happened. Stella picked up the television remote and decided some mindless TV would calm her down. She flipped the channels until she found a decent movie.

A few hours later, Ryan arrived home from work. He was covered in a light dusting of snow and his feet were white from walking to the house. He removed his shoes and placed them on the nearby heating vent to dry. Stella helped him remove his coat and gave him a welcome kiss.

"How was work?"

"About as boring as it usually is," Ryan said. "I am so glad I don't have to go back until after Christmas."

"Well, go change out of these wet clothes," Stella hung up his coat. "I'll get dinner ready. How does fish sound?"

"Delightful."

Ryan trudged up to the bedroom while Stella raided the refrigerator. She pulled out two frozen fish filets that she had already breaded. She pulled out a skillet and poured oil into it and warmed it on the stove. Once the fish was crackling in the skillet, Stella cut up vegetables for salads and washed some grapes. Ryan joined her and helped by setting the dining room table and pouring two glasses of milk. Stella flipped the fish in the skillet; it hissed in the oil. Once the fish was served on plates, they sat down to eat.

"Did I do a good job with the decorating?" Stella sliced up her fish and poured dressing on her salad.

"You always do a good job," Ryan took a bite of his fish. "Fish is good too."

"Thank you."

They chewed their food in pleasant silence. Roxanne weaved in and out of their feet, begging for a bite. Stella placed a piece of her fish onto her napkin and presented it to the cat, who ate it without tasting it. Stella looked out the patio window to see white powder falling from the sky.

"Looks like another snowstorm is coming."

Ryan jabbed at his salad, "It was a pain to drive in. I swear people forget how to drive in the snow. Do I really have to eat this?"

"It's good for you," Stella lectured. "Eat your grapes too."

"Yes, mother."

Ryan finished his food and helped Stella wash the dishes before retreating to the couch to watch the news on TV. Stella turned on all the Christmas lights and joined him. The weatherman on the television talked about another wave of snow coming to Ohio and warned drivers to be careful.

"No kidding," Ryan muttered. "I drove by at least five cars that had skidded off the road."

"I'm sure I would be one of them," Stella shuttered. "I am so bad at driving in the snow. I could be going as slow as possible and still end up in the ditch."

"Trust me, you are better than you think," Ryan wrapped an arm around his wife.

The news show then covered last-minute holiday shoppers and how stores were welcoming them with great deals. Stella was glad all her shopping was done. She hated waiting until the last minute to do anything, although she still felt bad about not getting presents for Jerot or Tuptup or even her grandmother. It was hard to buy things in Mayazure because she didn't have money there, and she couldn't buy anything on Earth and bring them with her. She knew that gifts weren't important; just being there was good enough, but Stella still felt bad about it.

Stella reached over and picked up the snow globe again. She tipped it over and made the snow fall inside. She tried not to think about the mysterious blonde woman and focused on the happy Santa inside. She remembered when she got the snow globe; her mother bought it for her a few Christmases ago. Seems like every year, someone always buys her a new Santa.

"You really like that thing, don't you?" Ryan had been watching.

"It brings me peace," Stella sighed. "Most of the time."

"How about now?"

"Of course," Stella put the snow globe back on the coffee table and kissed her husband. "Let's see what it's doing outside."

Stella got up and walked to the front window and pulled back the curtain. Though the sun had set long ago, Stella could see clearly with the Christmas lights, as well as the lights from the surrounding neighbors. The tiny front yard was packed with snow, at least two feet deep and more was falling. It fell in large clumps and accumulated on everything. The well-plowed road would soon be filled with snow again, but few people drove on their road anyway. Stella watched the snow for a good five minutes before Ryan joined her.

"Pretty, isn't it?" Ryan took her hand.

"It is when you don't have to drive in it."

"This is true."

Stella closed the curtains. She felt a slight chill from watching the outside, "I'm cold. I think I'm going to make some tea. Want some?"

"You bet," Ryan kissed Stella on the cheek and went back to the couch.

Stella went to the kitchen and put her grandmother's teakettle on the stove. As she pulled out the tea bags and mugs from the cupboard, Roxanne clawed at her pant leg, desperate for attention. Stella got out some cat food and put it down on the floor for the cat, and fixed her tea. She put sugar in the mugs and placed a tea bag in each. Stella stood and watched the teakettle. She could here the water faintly boiling inside. Once it started to whistle, Stella poured the hot water and let the teabags soak.

Stella called out to Ryan, "Did you really get all your shopping done this year, or are we going to have to go out tomorrow?" Ryan always waited until the last minute to do his Christmas shopping.

"Not this year. I'm done," was his reply.

"You bought everything you wanted to get for your parents?"

"Yep."

"What about for me?" Stella sounded doubtful.

"Of course." Ryan said, amused. "I would never forget you."

With the tea ready, Stella brought the mugs into the living room and handed one to Ryan before planting herself on the couch. Roxanne joined her.

"Well, good job then," Stella sipped her tea. "Too bad you can't be this organized every year."

"It was easy this year," Ryan blew across the top of his mug. He didn't like his tea as hot as Stella did. "The shopping in Vegas helped."

"Yes, you're right. I got all my shopping done there too," Stella smiled. "Except for you. I have to shop locally."

"Same here. Had to do it in secret," Ryan winked.

"Did you really wrap it all already?"

"You bet." Ryan grabbed the remote and flipped through the TV channels until he found his favorite sitcom. It entertained Stella while she drank her tea. The warm liquid soothed her insides and made her sleepy. She couldn't wait to go back to Mayazure, even if her grandmother and the citizens of Cobalian were in exile. None of the villagers seemed very worried about their situation. Perhaps it was Christmas cheer.

Stella finished her tea and waited for Ryan to finish before taking the mugs to the kitchen. She returned to the living room, "I'm tired. I think I'll go to bed," she said, kissing her husband good night.

Ryan looked at the clock hanging by the kitchen, "You don't have to go to bed now. We could stay up late and sleep in."

"I would love to, but I'm really tired."

"Okay, I'll probably go to bed soon too."

Stella made her way upstairs to the bedroom, followed by Roxanne. The cat found a spot on the bed to sleep, while Stella changed into her pajamas. She couldn't help but check her arm; her injury was now a thing of the past. Stella removed her glasses and put them on her dresser next to her silver jewelry box. She opened the box and found her grandmother's ring. As Stella put it on, it glimmered brightly in the artificial light of the room. Stella hopped into bed and closed her eyes. The last thing she remembered was gently petting Roxanne before falling into a deep sleep.

The Blonde Woman

Jerot paced eagerly in the Welcome Garden. He couldn't wait to see Stella. He rose early and set up equipment to practice archery. He had had no time to gather targets when Cobalian was invaded, so he had to improvise. He bought a few sacks of grain from Wreckton and painted targets on them. They weren't as nice as the targets at the armory tent, but a target was a target. They would have to do.

Stella appeared, somewhat happy to see Jerot this time, "Have you been waiting long?" Stella could tell he was anxious. Jerot handed her a cloak to protect her from the cold.

"It is just very dangerous to be out here. Stella Cinereous' guards sometimes patrol the pathway," he helped Stella onto his horse and led the Friesian out of the garden and down the pathway until they reached the fork. There, Jerot continued straight, cutting through the forest and trudging through the deep snow. Stella tried to look through the trees to see if she could glimpse at Cobalian but, even though the trees were bare, they blocked any sight of the city.

"I know this isn't the cheeriest of times," Stella said, "but do you have any plans for Christmas? It's only two days away."

"I have none," Jerot said. "I would imagine most of the villagers don't. We are all lucky just to be alive and to spend time with families."

Stella gave up trying to look through the trees. "A family is more important than presents."

"But I," Jerot hesitated, "have no family."

Stella was silent for a moment. She looked down from the horse and watched Jerot walk through the snow. The loss of Jerot's wife, Saura, was still a fresh wound. "That's not true. You can always spend time with me and Grandma."

Jerot stopped and looked up at Stella. His eyes shone, wet with tears and a smile formed across his lips. "I would love that, if you would have me."

"Absolutely. I bet we would have a great time."

Jerot started to walk again, leading the Friesian along with him. Stella shivered slightly in the cold and wrapped her cloak tighter around herself. They cut through Bondi Field when Stella had a thought.

"I'm surprised Radam is not with us. He is suppose to watch out for me. Mistis' orders, you know."

Jerot chuckled. "He wanted to come along, I assure you, but I felt he would get lost in all this snow. He trusted that I would look out for you until we reach the cave."

They walked along the makeshift path to the Cave of Eternal Blaze. At the foothills, a group of children played in the snow, watched by a few adults. Jerot waved to the chaperones before helping Stella off his horse. A crude stable had been erected at the bottom of the mountain. Jerot put his Friesian in one of the stalls before helping Stella up the rock stairs to the entrance of the cave. Radam was waiting for them at the large opening.

"You made it safely," he said.

"Of course," Jerot grabbed a lantern and lit it. "It's dangerous out there, but no one would dare challenge me."

"I was worried when I found out you disappeared," Radam pawed the ground, "The Queen explained to me about the ring you wear. That is some strange magic."

"Yes, it is a little weird," Stella looked at the ring. It reflected the light off of the lantern Jerot was holding. "I swear I am safe on Earth. You have no need to worry."

"I still wish I could go with you. I would feel better if I was at your side at all times."

"Shall we?" Jerot took Stella by the hand and they headed into the dark tunnel, followed closely by Radam. Stella could feel the coldness of Jerot's hand against hers, and her stomach jumped nervously. Once inside the cavern, Jerot extinguished the lantern and they made their way to the Queen's tent for breakfast. The Queen was outside the tent, sitting on a large blue pillow, talking to Tuptup while he cooked sausages over the fire.

"How is the weather out there?" asked Queen Iona. "I hope it isn't too cold for the children."

"It's cold," said Jerot, "but the children don't seem to mind."

"Good, good. I will send Tuptup to check on them after breakfast."

Tuptup chopped the cooked sausage finely and mixed it in a thick gravy. Stella helped pass out plates and biscuits and Tuptup poured the gravy. Stella sat down with her own plate and ate, picking out any large pieces of sausage and giving them to Radam to nibble on.

"Has there been any word from Stella the Subjugator?" Jerot asked between bites. "My knights grow anxious for battle."

"None, I'm afraid," Queen Iona offered a piece of sausage to Radam as well. "I will wait until after Christmas and then perhaps we will take the first step. My people cannot live here forever."

"Then I will tell my knights to continue training. I don't want them to be unprepared."

"Perhaps Mullitor will bring news," Queen Iona said. "I told him to fly over Cobalian while he is out hunting for breakfast." She changed the subject, "What would you like to do today, Stella?"

"I don't know. Watching the children play in the snow makes we want to join them. What do you say, Jerot?" Stella took a final bite of her gravy-soaked biscuit.

"That sounds like fun, but first I would like you to do some target practice," Jerot replied.

"Again?"

"You should be practicing everyday, so yes, again."

Tuptup gathered up the plates once everyone was done with breakfast. He then grabbed a cloak. "I will return shortly."

"Thank you, dear," Queen Iona smiled at the dwarf.

"Watch out for snowballs," Jerot called after him.

The Queen turned back to Stella. "I think those are great plans for this morning. You can meet me here for lunch and maybe we could work on some knitting later."

"What are you going to do this morning?" asked Stella.

The Queen reached under her pillow and pulled out a large book. "I manage to grab a few books before we fled Cobalian. They aren't much, but they might be useful in my little research project."

Stella smiled at the sight of the book. "Whatever entertains you, I guess."

Mullitor entered the cavern, coated lightly with snow. The Queen rose from her pillow as he made his way to her tent. "What news do you bring?"

"All is silent, I'm afraid," the dragon replied. "A few of the minotaurs tried to shoot me down with their meager arrows but, as far as I can see, there is no activity suggesting battle."

"Of course not," Stella said. "That witch got what she wanted. We have to take the first action to get Cobalian back."

"I agree," Jerot placed his hand on the hilt of his sword. "We can't just sit here and accept our fate."

"I am afraid you are both correct," said Queen Iona, "but let us not be hasty. It is the holidays and let us enjoy what we have. Then when the festivities are over, we shall send word to Stella Cinereous. I promise you, Jerot, there will be a battle."

Jerot smiled, "I want nothing more than to lop off some heads."

"Eww," Stella said with slight disgust. "But I want to help. Do you think I am good enough with the bow and arrow?"

"Absolutely not," Radam entered the conversation. "As your guardian, I refuse to let you be part of this battle."

Stella let out a sound of disappointment. "Mistis said I shouldn't fight Stella the Subjugator alone. She never said anything about not joining the battle."

"I think with more practice, you could become a member the archery team," Jerot said. "Archers are not part of the front line and are rarely injured in battle."

Stella turned to the Queen. "What do you think, grandma?"

The Queen thought for a moment, while everyone held their breath. Finally, she spoke, "I side with Radam, for I fear for your safety." Radam pawed the ground, celebrating his small victory. "But you are not a child, and you are free to make your own decisions."

"I can't just sit here and watch. I will join the other archers," Stella folded her arms, signaling her decision.

"Now wait a minute," Radam interjected. "I have no problem with you not becoming part of this fight."

"Sorry, Radam." Stella patted the cat on the head. "Looks like Mistis made you guard to a stubborn woman."

"Then let's not waste any more time," Jerot said. "We should go and practice and see if you are still good enough to help."

"You can come and watch, Radam," Stella turned to the cat. "Once you see how good I am, maybe you will change your mind."

"I would like to watch as well," added Mullitor.

"Great, it could be like a small party."

"As long as they don't impede your practicing," Jerot said.

"Of course not," the dragon said, reassuring him. "You won't even know Radam and I are there."

"Have a good time then," Queen Iona sat back down on her pillow and opened her book. "I will see you at lunch."

Jerot led the way through the cavern followed by Stella, Radam, and Mullitor bringing up the rear. They were a small parade that caught the attention of the villagers who waved and greeted them as they passed. They arrived at Jerot's camp, where Mullitor curled up in a small nook, out of the way, and Radam and Stella watched Jerot set up the targets. He dragged the sacks of grain out from behind his tent and lined them up against the cavern wall. Jerot then crawled into his tent and dug out his bow and a quiver full of arrows.

"Looks like we will have to share my bow," Jerot handed it to Stella. "I only had time to grab one before fleeing Cobalian."

Stella held up Jerot's bow. It was bigger and heavier than she was used to. "Let's give it a try," she pulled out an arrow from the quiver and lined it up against the bow.

She tried to remember everything Jerot taught her. She pulled back the string of the bow keeping in mind to not slouch her elbow. She inhaled deeply and as she breathed out, she let go of the arrow. It sailed straight to the middle target, hitting it just left of the bull's eye.

"Yay!" Radam cheered, standing on his hind legs and clapping his front paws together in applause.

"Good shot," added Mullitor.

Jerot turned and glared at the two spectators, "Quiet please."

"Sorry," Mullitor muttered. "It was a good shot though." Radam lowered his head in shame.

"Yes, it was," Jerot walked over and pulled the arrow out of the sack. "But let's try it again. Don't be afraid to take your time. These sacks aren't going to attack you, so you have plenty of time to make sure you have a good shot. An enemy will not always be right in front of you, so let's try the target on the right."

Stella set another arrow into Jerot's bow. She aimed at the sack of grain on the right, focusing on the center. After a minute of studying her target, she could feel the weight of the bow on her shoulders. Stella could hold the bow no longer and let go of the arrow, hitting below the bull's eye.

"Yay!" Radam said, more quietly.

"Another good shot, I would say," Mullitor whispered to the cat.

"Sorry," Stella adjusted her glasses. "Your bow is too heavy. I couldn't hold it up much longer."

"That's all right," Jerot pried the arrow out of the sack. "The weight is something you'll have to get used to. Now, try the target on the left."

For an hour Stella practiced her archery. Though the bow was heavy, she did quite well, but she still couldn't get the elusive bull's eye. Radam and Mullitor cheered quietly after each shot, giving Stella more and more confidence. Jerot finally decided that Stella had enough practice when the bags began to leak, spilling grain onto the cavern floor.

"Well, these targets are of no use now," he said. "Let's go see if anyone would like slightly-used bags of grain before we spill it everywhere."

Jerot picked up two of the bags and Stella grabbed the third. With

Mullitor and Radam following, they went from campsite to campsite, asking families if they would like any grain. Two small families split one of the bags, while two larger families took a bag each.

"This is wonderful," said one woman, "now I can make my Christmas bread. Thank you so much."

"You're welcome," Stella said.

"Let's head back to the Queen's tent," Jerot suggested. "I'm sure it's almost time for lunch."

"Yes, splendid idea," Mullitor licked his lips. "I am starting to get hungry. I could really go for a deer."

"Please don't tell me what you eat," Stella felt a little grossed out.

They headed to the Queen's tent, where Tuptup was busy cooking a large pot of stew. The Queen was sitting on her blue pillow, scribbling notes into the large book she was reading. Mullitor said his goodbyes before leaving to hunt for lunch.

The Queen placed her quill inside the book and closed it. "How was archery practice?"

"Okay," Stella sat down next to her grandmother. "Jerot's bow is too heavy, but I managed."

"I thought she did quite well," said Radam.

"Maybe Santa will get you your own bow," Queen Iona smiled.

"Oh, no that won't be necessary," Stella could sense her cheeks burning. She felt guilty that she could not get any of them any presents. "I don't need anything for Christmas."

"I understand. You shouldn't feel bad that you can not get us anything," Queen Iona said, "All I really want for Christmas is to spend time with you." This made Stella smile.

"The stew is ready," Tuptup handed out bowls and spoons. "I hope everyone is hungry." He poured stew into everyone's bowls and then strained out some of the beef and put it in a bowl for Radam.

The stew smelled wonderful, full of potatoes, carrots, celery and peas.

Stella spooned out a potato and chewed it slowly, savoring the flavor. Jerot ate his stew so fast that he had seconds before anyone else. No one spoke as the stew occupied them. Before Stella finished her second helping, Mullitor returned. He seemed hurried and nervous.

"Your majesty," he addressed the Queen. "There are three travelers coming up the path. Two are minotaurs and one is a cloaked figure on horseback. I believe it is a messenger from Stella Cinereous."

"All right, some action," Jerot stood up with excitement.

"Now now," Queen Iona arose from her pillow and placed a hand on Jerot's shoulder. "Such a small group is no sign of an invasion. Let us go and meet them at the foot of the mountain and see what this messenger has to tell us."

"Is there anything else I can do?" Mullitor asked.

"No, you just stay inside," Queen Iona wrapped herself in a cloak while Tuptup passed out cloaks to Stella and

Jerot. "We wouldn't want to scare them away."

Jerot led the way out of the cavern, followed by the Queen, Tuptup, Stella and Radam. They made their way down the icy stairway to the foot of the mountain. There, children still played in the snow.

Tuptup approached one of the chaperones, a young woman. "It's best you get these young'uns inside. We have visitors from the enemy." The woman nodded and told the other adults, who then herded the children up to the cave.

They stood at the base of the mountain, waiting for any movement from the path up ahead. Stella's feet were starting to get cold and Radam shivered, almost buried in the snow. Tuptup picked up Radam and wrapped the cat inside his cloak.

"Thank you, dear friend," Radam sounded relieved. "This is no time to be unprotected." Tuptup went to speak, but Jerot raised his hand, signaling silence. They all looked to see three figures coming up the path.

Mullitor's description had indeed been accurate. Two of the travelers were large minotaurs, one was white with patches of brown in his fur, while the other was as black as night. They were dressed in red armor and armed with swords and shields bearing the insignia of a red bird. They stood on either side of a white horse which carried the third traveler, who was wearing a red cloak, the hood covering its face. All three stopped a few feet from the Queen and her company.

Jerot took a step forward. "I am Jerot Catosan, Lead Knight of Cobalian and of Queen Iona Bale and I demand to know your reason for coming here." The black minotaur snorted and stamped his hoofed foot on the ground. Stella could see snot running from his nose and was slightly disgusted.

The cloaked figure spoke, "I am in search of something that belongs to Iona Bale." The voice was that of a woman who spoke smoothly and without falter.

"That's *Queen* Iona Bale to you," snapped Tuptup, "and whatever it is you or that wretched princess is looking for you can't have it."

"Is that so?" The woman removed her hood and everyone gasped. Stella looked in shock, for there in front of her was the blonde woman she had seen in visions of her reflection. Finally she was looking at this woman, who truly existed.

She was more beautiful in person. Her long blonde hair shone in the winter sun and her blue eyes were large and stunning against her high cheekbones. Her lips were painted ruby red and, even though she was covered in a cloak, Stella could tell she had a slender body.

"Who is that?" Stella leaned and whispered to Tuptup.

"That is Stella Cinereous herself," Tuptup whispered back. "How bold for her to venture out without her army. Whatever she wants, it must be important."

"It is good to see you," Queen Iona smiled, as if she was seeing an old friend.

"It is?" Jerot asked, but the Queen ignored him.

"What is it you need?"

Stella the Subjugator glared down at the Queen. "I have torn your castle apart in search of something of importance. Something I know that has great power. I want it and I will do anything to acquire it."

"Well, out with it then," Tuptup's impatience grew. "Unless you want us to stand in the snow all day and guess what it is."

"Quiet, dwarf!" barked the brown and white minotaur, making Stella Cinereous laugh. No one else found it funny.

"What I want," Stella the Subjugator became serious again, "is your gold ring; the one with the diamond in it. I hear it can take you to other worlds. I want it so I can conquer more than just Mayazure."

"Oh that," Stella spoke causing everyone to turn their attention towards her, "I'm afraid you can't have it."

The blonde woman looked down her nose at Stella. "And why not?"

"Because I have it," Stella held up her right hand revealing her grandmother's ring. The diamond glittered, as if mocking Stella Cinereous.

The blonde woman's eyes widened in disdain. "Who are you? What makes you think you can possess that ring?"

"I am Stella Tyrian, granddaughter of Queen Iona Bale."

Stella the Subjugator turned her face in disgust, but then gave out a shrill laugh, "You are nothing. You are a descendant of some woman who was appointed queen simply because the townspeople chose her, not because she conquered Cobalian. I come from fifteen generations of royalty who earned our reputation for being forceful and feared."

"Not to mention inbreeding," muttered Jerot, causing Stella to cover her mouth to stifle her laughter.

"I have come out of ruin, and established a new era of the Cinereous blood line," Stella the Subjugator continued. "I have taken over Cobalian and it now belongs to me… including that ring. I am more deserving of it."

"How so?" Queen Iona still smiled pleasantly.

"Just look at me," Stella Cinereous grinned evilly. "I am more beautiful and wealthy than your descendant," she flipped her long golden hair. "I have servants who spend hours on my hair to make it perfect," she stared down at Stella. "You have stringy hair that is a horrid shade of brunette."

"There's nothing wrong with my hair," Stella said, but the blonde woman continued.

"What are those things on your face? They make you look like an owl."

"They're called glasses," Stella reached up and touched her frames. "I need them to see."

Stella the Subjugator laughed, "Ugly and blind, not to mention you look like you eat the main share of food."

"I'm not fat," Stella could feel her face burning with rage. "I am just the right weight. You are too skinny."

Stella Cinereous laughed again. "There is no such thing as being too thin, little piggy."

"Enough!" Jerot shouted. He could no longer take the abuse of his Stella. Any insult to her was an insult to Saura. "You had your fun, but you are getting nowhere. You will not get that ring."

"Perhaps we can settle this on the battlefield," Queen Iona said. Stella could see a burning in her blue eyes.

"Now you are speaking my language," Stella Cinereous beamed with delight.

"Your army against mine. If I win, then you must give back Cobalian."

"And if I win, then all of Cobalian is mine, including that ring."

"Shall we battle in a week's time?" Queen Iona smiled pleasantly, as if she was planning a tea party. "We can settle this before the New Year."

"A week is plenty of time for me," Stella the Subjugator seemed pleased. "We will do battle on the southern side of Chamoisee Canyon."

"That sounds dangerous," Jerot spoke to the Queen.

"Not at all," Queen Iona replied. "The Canyon is flat and there is barely any snow there." She turned to the blonde woman, "Chamoisee Canyon sounds like a splendid location. Do you prefer sunrise or sunset?"

"An hour before sunset," Stella Cinereous replied. "The battle will go faster that way."

"Agreed," Queen Iona said. "Nothing is more annoying than a battle that lasts all day."

"Very well," Stella the Subjugator pulled the hood over her head. "I bid you farewell until a week's time has passed." She turned her horse to leave, followed by the two minotaurs, and headed back down the path.

"Bye bye, now," Queen Iona called, waving at them as if to old friends. Once the three travelers were gone, the Queen turned to Jerot, her face serious. "Gather up your knights and prepare them for battle. Then go to Wreckton and see if there are any supplies and weaponry the goblins will be willing to sell us."

"Yes, ma'am," Jerot bolted up the rock stairway to the cave.

The Queen then turned to Tuptup. "Write out a decree that we will need all able bodies to join my army. We will need everyone we can get."

"You got it," Tuptup handed Radam to Stella and followed Jerot up to the cave.

"What can I do?" Stella was eager to be of assistance. There was no way she was going to sit by and let Stella Cinereous take everything.

The Queen's smile returned. She place her hand on Stella's shoulder. "I think you and I should get out of this cold and have some nice hot tea."

"Sounds like a good idea to me," Radam kneaded Stella's arm and purred softly.

"But I want to help," said Stella, as they made their way up the rocky path.

"And you will," the Queen reassured her. "But you have had enough archery practice today. Let's just enjoy some time together and wait for Tuptup to finish that decree."

At the entrance of the cave, Stella put Radam down and grabbed a lantern. They made their way through the dark tunnel and into the cavern, where they met Jerot and Mullitor.

"We're off to Wreckton," Jerot said. "Any other last minute instructions?"

"None, dear," Queen Iona said, "except have a safe trip."

"Can I come?" Stella was insistent on helping.

Jerot smiled and ran his hand through Stella's hair. "Maybe next time when we aren't on official business."

"Okay, be careful."

"We will," said Mullitor. He gently nudged Stella with his snout as Jerot climbed onto his back.

"Bye, bye," Queen Iona and Stella waved as Mullitor carried Jerot into the tunnel and disappeared into the darkness.

"Now," Queen Iona placed the teakettle on the fire before settling down onto her blue pillow. "What kind of tea would you like?"

"Whatever you're having is fine," Stella sat down on another blue pillow. Radam curled up in a ball next to her. "I feel weird sitting here, doing nothing."

"We could work on that knitting."

"No, that's not what I meant," Stella shook her head. "I want to help with the battle."

"Patience, my child," Queen Iona said. "You mustn't rush these things." They sat on their pillows sipping tea when, finally, the Queen spoke again. "Planning a battle is not hard work. Most of the time will be spent on gathering people up to fight and giving them time to prepare."

"Do you really think a week is enough time?" Stella asked.

The Queen lowered her head, "When I say 'prepare,' I don't mean practice. You have to understand that many who fight will not come home."

"You mean they must prepare to die?" Radam said, giving Stella a concerned look. "You really should reconsider this."

This realization saddened Stella at first, then it frightened her. "Perhaps I shouldn't fight in this battle. What happens if I die here?"

"I am not sure of that answer," Queen Iona finished her tea. "But, as I have said before, your choice to join the fight is entirely up to you."

Stella stared into her teacup before looking out at the campsites in the cavern. She watched as men and women played with their children, enjoyed a late lunch, or rested by the fire. Which of these people were going to die for their queen? She felt her grandmother rest a hand on her shoulder.

"It is a part of life," Queen Iona said. "A tough one, but inevitable."

"I might have to rethink about fighting."

"You do that," Queen Iona smiled. "You have a week to decide."

Tuptup emerged out of the large tent with a piece of parchment in his hand, "I have arranged the decree for you."

"Let's hear it," said Queen Iona.

Tuptup cleared his throat and read aloud from the parchment:

> *"This decree hereby calls all males of adult age to report to any knight for battle against Stella Cinereous. This call is mandatory. Any women who wish to join the call may do so, but it is optional. The battle will be held a week from today at the Chamoisee Canyon, one hour before sunset. Please bring any weaponry you have. If you have no weaponry, it will be provided for you."*

"Sounds good to me," Radam said, licking his paw.

"Yes, I agree," said Queen Iona. "Make several copies, put my seal on them and post them around the cavern."

Tuptup nodded and disappeared inside the tent. Stella finished her tea and proceeded to scratch Radam behind the ears, which caused him to purr with enjoyment.

"I suppose since there's nothing else that can be done, we might as well get some knitting done," Stella said.

"That's the ticket," Queen Iona stood up and stretched. "I'll get the yarn." The Queen went inside her tent and soon emerged with a basket full of yarn. "Let's work on the double seed stitch today."

"Okay," Stella grabbed a pair of needles and watched as her grandmother knit and purled the yarn to make the stitch. Stella tried the stitch herself, but the thought of the impending battle distracted her and she just couldn't do it correctly. "Dang."

"That's all right," said Queen Iona. "You'll get it eventually."

Stella continued to try but, after an hour, she gave up and switched to the simpler garter stitch. Radam enjoyed playing with the yarn as it moved around the floor.

Tuptup appeared with a stack of parchments. "Well, I'm off."

"Thank you, dear," said Queen Iona without looking up from her knitting.

Stella became bored with knitting and played with Radam, dragging the yarn around for him to chase. The Queen managed to knit a pair of mittens before Jerot and Mullitor returned.

"Welcome back," Queen Iona beamed.

"Thank you," Jerot said, brushing the snow off of his cloak. "I've got to go get the other knights. I have several crates to drag in." He disappeared down the cavern.

"Did you have a good flight?" Stella stood up from her pillow and patted Mullitor on his snout. He purred from her touch.

"The snow is starting to come down again, but it is nothing I can't handle." Mullitor bared his teeth in a smile. "How is the decree coming along? Jerot told me about what happened between you and Stella the Subjugator."

"Being distributed as we speak," Queen Iona packed away the yarn, much to Radam's disappointment. "I'd better go find my purse. I'm sure I owe Jerot for the supplies." She entered the tent.

Jerot returned with twenty of his best knights. Stella follow them to the tunnel. "Let me help."

Jerot smiled at her eagerness, "I think these crates might be a little heavy for you."

"I'm not a weakling."

"Well, I'm sure I can find something for you to do," Jerot lit a lantern and he led Stella and the other knights down the tunnel.

When they came to the entrance, Stella saw a large net sitting on the ledge. Jerot handed Stella the lantern and, with his sword, cut the net open to reveal ten large crates. Two knights handled each crate and Jerot gathered up the net.

"All right," Jerot said to Stella. "Lead us back through the tunnel." With the lantern held high, Stella guided the way, followed by the twenty knights with their crates, Jerot bringing up the rear. Once back in the glow of the cavern, Stella put out the lantern and set it down by the tunnel. "Good job," Jerot smiled at Stella. He turned to the knights. "All right, men, take those to the supply tent." The knights did as ordered.

Jerot and Stella went to the Queen's tent, where she was waiting with Radam and Mullitor. She was holding a large navy blue bag, embroidered with a white heart.

"What do I owe you dear?" Queen Iona asked.

"No, no, that won't be necessary," Jerot waved his hand in rejection. "I have plenty of coin to spare."

"Nonsense," Queen Iona reached into her bag. "I will not have you spend your own money for the people of Cobalian."

Jerot hesitated before answering. "Very well, you owe me five hundred gold."

"I thought it was seven hundred," said Mullitor. Jerot shot him a look, which made Stella and Radam laugh.

"How about I give you six hundred and we'll call it even," Queen Iona said through her giggles.

While The Queen and Jerot counted out gold, Tuptup returned, no longer holding any parchments. "The decree has been posted, as ordered," he said.

"Wonderful," said Queen Iona. "Once I'm done here, we can have dinner."

"I'll get that started," Tuptup made his way to the tent.

"Do you need help?" Stella asked.

"Not yet, but I'll let you know."

"Hmm, dinner sounds like a good idea," Mullitor licked his lips. "All that flying has made me hungry. I will be back shortly."

"Happy hunting," Radam said, as Mullitor took his leave.

After Jerot was paid, he took a seat on one of the pillows and propped his feet up on a green crystal. The Queen sat down also. Tuptup came out of the tent, carrying an assortment of bags and a frying pan. He handed Stella a box of matches.

"Be a good girl and relight the fire for me," he said. As he headed back to the tent, the Queen held out her purse to him.

"Can you put that away for me?" Queen Iona asked the dwarf.

"Will do."

Soon, the fire was lit and pork chops simmered in the frying pan. Radam sat close to the fire, licking his lips with anticipation.

"Don't sit too close or you'll burn your nose clean off," Tuptup said.

"I can't help it," the cat replied. "I didn't realize how hungry I was until I smelled this."

"Me neither," said Stella.

After dinner, Tuptup cleared away the dishes with Stella's help. Inside the tent was a small sink. The Minots used water stored in large canteens to wash the dishes, and dried them with a towel.

"The trick is to use as little water as possible," Tuptup said. "Just enough to clean everything."

While the Minots worked, Stella and Tuptup went outside. Mullitor had come back from hunting, but he was not the only new arrival at the Queen's campsite. Several of the townspeople had come, looking for Jerot, asking about the decree and reporting for battle. Jerot waved his hands to calm them and get their attention.

"If you will just follow me," he said, "we can head to the supply tent were we will assign you to positions and weaponry." Jerot made his way through the crowd and they followed.

"Are they upset?" Stella asked her grandmother.

"Oh, no," Queen Iona smiled, "they are eager to fight. My people are not afraid to exchange blows in the name of Cobalian."

"I'm glad someone isn't afraid," Radam twitched his nose. "I'm scared out of my wit's end of the whole thing."

Stella watched the people follow Jerot, still unsure of her involvement in this battle. "I'm a little scared too, Radam," she said.

While they waited for Jerot to return, Tuptup got out a guitar and strummed a few tunes to entertain the Queen. Stella didn't know any of the songs, but clapped along to the music. Radam howled merrily while Mullitor sang in a heavy bass. With the Queen singing as well, they made a strange trio. By the time Jerot returned, the campfire was burning low and contentment filled the air.

"Is everything alright?" Queen Iona asked her knight.

"Oh yes," Jerot said. "They are an enthusiastic bunch, but everything seems to be in order." Jerot eyed Tuptup's guitar. "Play *Green Eyes of Spring*, that's my favorite."

"Ah, now that is a wonderful song," Mullitor said.

Tuptup began to play, as Jerot offered a hand to Stella. "Shall I have this dance?" he asked. Stella gave him her hand and he pulled her up off her pillow. The Queen, Radam and Mullitor sang while Jerot spun Stella around the campsite.

> *I once knew a girl with lips of red*
> *And golden curls upon her head*
> *Her skirt would sway and it would swing*
> *But what I love the most was her Green Eyes of Spring*

Jerot twirled Stella around in his arms making her laugh and forget her troubles, even for just a moment. He dipped her low as the second verse continued.

> *I gave her flowers and I gave her stones*
> *I gave her poems that were my own*
> *But I couldn't give her a diamond ring*
> *I was not the only one who loved her Green Eyes of Spring*

Jerot was such a smooth dancer and Stella could feel his strength as he cradled her. She became lost in his eyes and didn't even hear the rest of the song.

> *I gave her my soul and I gave her my heart*
> *But she took all these gifts and she tore them apart*
> *She had promised her love to the son of the King*
> *And I never saw again the girl with Green Eyes of Spring*

Everyone applauded at Jerot and Stella's dancing; the clapping broke Stella from her spell, and she blushed from all the attention.

"Bravo," said Queen Iona, "very well done." Jerot bowed low.

"Yes," Mullitor added, "marvelous dancing."

"Thank you, thank you," Jerot said.

"Well, that was a splendid evening," Queen Iona yawned. "But it seems to be time for bed."

"Already?" Stella didn't feel the slightest bit tired.

"I'm afraid so."

Tuptup stretched and yawned as well. "Aye, all this playing has made me sleepy."

Jerot took Stella's hands in his. "I guess I will bid you farewell for the night," he kissed Stella on the cheek and she felt her insides flutter. Jerot waved goodbye to everyone before heading to his own tent.

"I also shall say goodnight," said Mullitor, and he headed deeper into the cavern to find a place to sleep.

The Queen, Stella, Tuptup and Radam went inside the Queen's tent to prepare for bed. Radam nestled down with the Minots in their nest of tunics, while Stella changed into her pink nightgown. She laid down on the cot and looked at her grandmother's ring. Stella felt torn; should she fight along with the others in battle, or not? On one hand, she had to worry about her safety, but, on the other hand, it was her ring now, and she should do whatever it took to defend it. Stella sighed deeply and continued to stare at the ring. Then she felt a hand rest upon her shoulder. She turned to see her grandmother looking down at her.

"Still unsure?" Queen Iona asked.

"Very," was Stella's reply.

"Do not worry. The decision will come to you. For now, just rest." The Queen kissed Stella on the forehead before retiring to her own cot. Stella closed her eyes and drifted into a deep sleep.

The First Holiday

After a few days without any significant events, Stella awoke on Christmas Day. Her alarm buzzed with slight annoyance and she turned it off. Stella rolled over to see Ryan, still snoring faintly, beside her. She gently poked him in the side and he snorted in response. With a sigh, Stella pulled herself out of bed and opened the bedroom door, greeted by Roxanne. The cat meowed with a happy tone and rubbed against Stella's leg as she headed down to the kitchen. Without thinking, Stella fed Roxanne and made herself a bowl of cereal. The cold milk woke her up, and she felt better after the bowl was empty.

Stella took a quick shower and dressed into jeans and a red sweater. Again she poked at Ryan, still asleep in bed. He grunted and rolled over. Stella shook her head and went back down to the kitchen. She had to prepare for her guests, who were to arrive around lunchtime.

Stella opened the refrigerator and checked on the food. The frozen shrimp was thawing nicely and the cookies she baked yesterday were nice and cold. Stella took out all the vegetables and began to wash them. She cut them up into bite-size pieces and arranged them on a green glass platter. In the center of the vegetable artwork, she placed a small bowl of spinach dip, and then put the whole platter back into the refrigerator.

Stella pulled out potatoes and a large bag of shredded cheese. She washed and cut the potatoes into slices, poured them into her crock-pot, sprinkled on the cheese and mixed them. As she plugged in the crock-pot, she heard faint footsteps from above, followed by the rushing noise of water. Ryan was taking a shower.

Stella took out the cookies and rearranged them on a clear platter before placing them back into the refrigerator. She couldn't help but taste one, a Kifli cookie with apricot filling. She smiled with satisfaction at her handiwork. As Stella assembled the shrimp on a green platter, Ryan came trudging down the stairs, still half asleep. He wore jeans and a green sweater, which Stella picked out for him the night before. It made them look well coordinated.

"Good morning," Stella smiled, putting a small bowl of cocktail sauce in the middle of the shrimp platter, "and Merry Christmas."

Ryan mumbled a Merry Christmas in return and opened the refrigerator. He grabbed a cinnamon cookie off the platter and drank straight out of the juice carton, which annoyed Stella. Ryan put the juice carton back and reached for a second cookie.

"No," Stella commanded.

"Oh, come on!" Ryan moaned. "There are plenty here."

"No," repeated Stella, turning on the oven. "Why don't you get the ham ready for me, please."

Ryan sighed and, pulled out the large ham and a jar of cherry glaze from the refrigerator. He carefully took off the wrapping and placed the ham in the roasting pan. Ryan poured the glaze over the ham, gently smoothing it out with a spoon until he was pleased with his masterpiece.

"Does this need to go in now?" Ryan asked.

"Yes," Stella said as she split up buns and piled them into a large glass bowl. "The oven should be ready by now."

Ryan slid the roasting pan into the oven before slamming the door shut. "Anything else you need?"

"Not in here," Stella placed a napkin over the buns. "Go see if the driveway needs shoveling."

Ryan groaned, "I had to ask."

Ryan slipped on his boots and coat, and went out the front door.

Stella rinsed out the empty glaze jar and threw it in the recycle bin next to the trashcan.

"Let's see," she muttered to herself. "Ham, cookies, potatoes, shrimp, veggies, buns … what am I missing?" Stella continued to mutter food while Roxanne watched her from underneath the dining room table. Stella thought long and hard before it clicked. "Green bean casserole!" she exclaimed.

Stella reached in the pantry cupboard and grabbed a couple cans of green beans, mushroom soup and a container of French fried onions. She poured the ingredients into a baking pan, added milk to the mixture and placed the pan into the refrigerator, to bake later. Roxanne caught sight of the milk jug and begged for some.

"Okay, okay," Stella poured some milk into a small bowl and put it on the floor for the cat. Roxanne made guttering slurping sounds as she lapped away. Stella just shook her head and made her way to the front door, where she put on her boots and coat before going outside to join her husband.

About two inches of fresh snow had fallen during the night. Ryan was busy pushing the snow out of the driveway; he had already removed the snow around their two vehicles. Stella grabbed the broom that was propped by the front door and swept off the porch and the stairs. A bag of salt was also by the front door. Stella reached in and pulled out a cup-full of salt and threw it on the porch.

"You need help?" Stella called out to Ryan.

"No, no," Ryan rested his elbow on the handle of the shovel. "I'm about half done. Shouldn't take much longer."

"Okay," Stella went inside and removed her coat and boots. Stella filled the sink with soapy water and washed dishes. There weren't many, but it was better to do them now and get them out of the way. It also made the house look more organized. The warm water running over Stella's cold hands filled her whole body with warmth. Each dish was set into the drying rack, and she finished by wiping down the countertops.

Stella heard Ryan come through the front door. He came into the kitchen, his cheeks red from the chilling wind outside.

"You haven't seen the newspaper while you were out there, did you?"

"No paper today," Stella said, putting a bowl in the cupboard. "It's a holiday."

Ryan smacked himself on the forehead, which made Stella giggle. "I knew that."

"Uh huh," Stella couldn't help but smile, "sure you did."

Ryan grabbed a second towel out of a drawer and helped dry the rest of the dishes. After the last dish was put away, Stella reached into the closet for the broom and dustpan.

"I'm going to sweep this floor," she said. "Can you straighten up the couch covers in the living room?"

"No problem," Ryan disappeared.

"And pick up any clumps of cat hair you see off the carpet, while you're in there,"

"Okay," Stella heard Ryan call from the living room.

Stella ran the broom over the kitchen floor, humming a tune as she went. She moved around the floor as if she was still dancing with Jerot, his favorite song still resonating in her ears. Though he wasn't there, she could feel his arms around her and she could see his face when she closed her eyes. Stella snapped herself out of her daydream and finished the floor. Ryan came in and tossed a handful of cat hair in the trash can.

"Anything else?" he asked.

"Did you make the bed?"

Ryan wrinkled up his face. "No, but I will."

"All right, do that and then you're free," Stella kissed him.

"If you need me, I'll be in my office. Just going to check my e-mail," and Ryan vanished upstairs.

Stella looked at the clock on the kitchen wall. It was still an hour and a

half before her guests would arrive.
Her mother and father would be here
on time, as they always were, but her
Aunt Shelly and Uncle Dominic
would arrive fashionably late. For
some reason, they were never
punctual.

Stella set the dining room table. It
really was only meant to seat four, but
six people could fit comfortably. She
arranged the chairs and put on a deep
green tablecloth. Stella opened one of
the kitchen cupboards and produced
six deep red cloth napkins, which she
placed on the table. She opened the
china cabinet and took out her best
silverware. They had deep red handles
that matched the cloth napkins. She
also took out six wine glasses and six
water glasses and set them on the
table as well. Stella then gently pulled
out her most precious items: the china
that once belonged to her
grandmother. Each piece was white,
rimmed with gold and adorned by a
single pink rose. They didn't match
the rest of the table settings, but it
didn't matter. Everyone who would be

there today knew this china and
expected it to be used today. She laid
out six large plates and six side plates.

Stella again glanced at the clock. It
was about time to put in the casserole.
She made her way to the kitchen and
was struck by the smell of the ham,
slowly cooking in the oven. Roxanne
was patiently sitting in front of the
oven, watching it with unblinking
eyes. Stella took the green bean
casserole out of the refrigerator.

"Excuse me," Stella looked down
at the cat and gently nudged Roxanne
away from the oven with her foot, "I
need to get in here." Stella opened the
oven door and placed the casserole
next to the ham. "Okay, carry on,"
Stella patted Roxanne on the head and
proceeded into the living room.

Ryan was gathering all the
magazines off the coffee table, "I'm
going to take these upstairs."

"Thank you," said Stella.

"What do you want to do with the
snow globe?" Ryan pointed to the
glass orb with the cheery Santa inside.

"Just leave it. I'm sure there will be plenty of room for it."

"Okay. Turn on the TV and see if the parade is still going on. I'll be right back."

Stella plopped down on the couch and turned on the television, using the remote control to flip through the channels until she found the Christmas parade. Ryan soon joined her and they watched the elaborate floats and occasional music performance or marching band. Every so often, Stella would peek at the clock. When she saw that her guests would be arriving in fifteen minutes, she decided it was time to bring out the hors d'oeuvres.

"Want to help me with the appetizers?" Stella turned to her husband.

"Of course," Ryan beamed, "as long as I can have another cookie."

They entered into the kitchen and Stella removed the vegetable tray, shrimp tray and the plate of cookies. They set everything down on the coffee table; there was plenty of room for the snow globe.

"Is that all?" Ryan reached for his cookie.

"Mom is bringing fudge, but there should still be enough room." Stella picked up a carrot and popped it into her mouth.

Roxanne took her attention away from the oven to wander into the living room where she stared at the plate of shrimp. She licked her lips and, when she thought no one was looking, slid a paw up to try and steal one.

"No, no," Stella scooped up the four-legged ball of fur, "bad kitty!" She grabbed a shrimp off the tray. "Come on, I'll let you eat one out of your dish," and she carried the cat into the kitchen.

Stella put Roxanne down, took a knife out of the drawer and cut up the shrimp into bite-sized pieces. Roxanne mewed and pawed at Stella's leg as she put the shrimp on a small plate and set it on the floor. Roxanne chewed with slurping noises, making Stella shake her head.

"How did I raise such a pig?" she gently ran her hand down the cat's back before returning to the living room.

Ryan was standing at the window, looking out. "I think your parents are here."

"Awesome," Stella turned off the television and went to the front door. She opened it just as her mom and dad walked up the front steps.

"Hello" Celeste said cheerfully as she walked over the threshold. She was carrying a large covered plate. "And Merry Christmas."

"Merry Christmas," Stella kissed her mother before taking the plate from her. "I'm guessing this is the fudge."

"Oh, yes. I made three different kinds." Celeste handed her coat and hat to Ryan.

Stella turned to her father, who was holding a large stack of presents. She kissed him, "Merry Christmas."

"Merry Christmas, princess," Ferdinand said.

"Just put those gifts by the tree," Stella waved her hand toward the Christmas tree. Her father complied, before removing his own coat and handing it to Ryan.

Stella took the fudge to the kitchen and uncovered it. There was plain, one with chopped peanuts and peanut butter fudge. Stella carried the fudge into the living room and placed it on the coffee table with the rest of the appetizers. Ferdinand and Ryan were already loading their paper plates with food, while Celeste sat in the rocking chair that had belonged to her mother.

"Anyone want anything to drink?" Stella reached for a piece of the plain fudge for herself.

"No, I'm good," Ferdinand said while chewing on a piece of shrimp.

"I'll have some tea," said Celeste.

Stella nodded and went back into the kitchen. She put the teakettle on the stove and grabbed a mug from the cupboard. Stella put a spoonful of sugar and placed a tea bag into the mug. She knew exactly how her mother liked her tea. Roxanne returned to the kitchen at the sight of the milk and began to beg again.

"I don't think so," Stella put the cap back on the milk jug and slid it into the refrigerator, much to the cat's protest., "Now shoo, you little glutton."

Roxanne instead followed Stella into the living room. She handed the tea to her mother. Celeste smiled and sipped the tea.

"Thank you," she said, "it's perfect." Roxanne jumped into Celeste's lap and tried to stick her nose into the mug. "You don't like tea." Celeste petted the cat and tried to keep the mug out of her reach.

Stella grabbed a plate and filled it with hors d'oeuvres before taking a seat next to Ryan. "How was the traffic, Dad? I hope the roads weren't too bad."

"Nah, nothing I can't handle," Ferdinand said as he helped himself to more food, "There weren't too many cars on the road."

"Don't eat too much," Celeste lectured her husband. "You won't have room for the main meal."

"I always have plenty of room," Ferdinand patted his stomach, which was surprisingly trim for his age. He was notorious for eating too much, yet never gained a pound.

Stella finished her plate of food before getting up to look out the window. There was no sign of her aunt and uncle.

"Don't worry. You know they are always late," Celeste said without taking her eyes off the cat.

"I know, but I don't want my food to burn either," Stella straightened the curtains before taking her seat again.

"It won't," Stella's mother finished her tea. "A few extra minutes in the oven isn't going to hurt anything."

"I can take that for you."

"No no, you just sat down," Celeste put the empty mug on the floor next to the rocking chair. Roxanne immediately jumped down and tried to stick her head into it.

"Dear God," Ryan said, "you'd think we don't feed her or something." Ferdinand laughed as Celeste pushed the cat away, with no success.

Stella heard the faint sound of a door slam from outside. "I bet that's them." She went to the window to have a peek. "Yep, they're here." Stella took her place at the front door and Ryan joined her.

Stella opened the door for her Aunt Shelly and Uncle Dominic. Shelly looked very much like her sister; thin with graying hair, but shoulder-length, unlike Celeste's hair which was cropped short. Dominic always reminded Stella of Santa Claus. He had a long gray beard and a big potbelly.

"Merry Christmas!" Shelly said. She hugged both Stella and Ryan. "I know I wasn't supposed to bring anything, but I baked some extra cookies and thought I should share."

She handed a covered plate to Stella, while Ryan took her coat.

"You can never have too many cookies," said Ryan.

Dominic set down by the tree a large bag filled with Christmas presents before removing his own coat. "Sorry we're late. I had a little glue mishap with my Corsair." Dominic worked on model airplanes as a hobby.

"That's quite all right," Stella said, as she transplanted the new cookies onto the platter, "we were just nibbling on the appetizers."

Shelly and Dominic settled onto the couch and helped themselves to the hors d'oeuvres, while Stella grabbed Ryan and pulled him into the kitchen.

"I'm going to need your help," she said.

"But," Ryan whined, "there are more cookies."

"You will have plenty of time for cookies, but first I need you." Stella opened the oven and, with potholders, removed the ham and the green bean casserole. "Put the casserole on the table, please," she instructed Ryan. Stella carefully lifted the ham from the roasting pan and put it on a platter from her grandmother's china. When Ryan returned, she handed him the china platter to put on the table as well.

Next Stella opened the crock-pot of cheesy potatoes. She scooped them out onto a large bowl and walked them into the dining room, catching Ryan as he sampled a piece of ham.

"Really?" she asked. "You can't wait a few more minutes?"

"I was just checking to make sure it was good," Ryan swallowed quickly. "We wouldn't want to poison are guests."

Stella rolled her eyes. "Go get the buns, please," she said, shoving him back into the kitchen.

Ryan grabbed the bowl of buns while Stella rummaged in the refrigerator for condiments. She found the ketchup, mustard and mayonnaise and set them on the dining table next to the buns.

"How does it look?" Stella asked.

"Looks delicious," Ryan reached for another piece of ham, but Stella smacked his hand away.

"Behave."

Stella entered the living room where her guests were enjoying a pleasant conversation. Uncle Dominic was explaining the challenge of placing decals on his model airplanes. "You have to rub them down quickly or you get air bubbles trapped underneath," he said, "a whole plane can be ruined by poor decal placement."

Stella cleared her throat to get everyone's attention, "Lunch is ready."

"Oh, wonderful," said Celeste as everyone gathered into the dining room.

As the guests took their seats, Stella took drink requests. "We have milk, iced tea, Pepsi, ginger ale, orange juice and wine.

"I'll take some milk," said Celeste.

"Me too," answered Stella's father.

"I'll think I will have some wine," Dominic said.

"Just water for me," Shelly handed over her glass.

"You take care of the wine," Stella directed her husband, "I'll get the rest."

While Ryan fumbled with the wine bottle, Stella filled the glasses. She placed ice in three of the glasses and filled one with water and the other two with Pepsi (for herself and Ryan). Stella filled the remaining two with milk. By the time she was done, Ryan had successfully opened the wine and poured it into the wine glass.

As they carried the glasses back to their guests, everyone had already filled their plates with warm food. Stella and Ryan sat down at the table and served themselves.

"Who would like to say grace?" Stella asked.

"I will," Dominic cleared his throat while everyone bowed their heads. "Dear Lord," he started, "thank you for this wonderful meal we are about to partake, and thank you for giving us the opportunity to meet together to celebrate the birth of your son. In Jesus' name we pray, Amen."

"Amen," added Celeste.

Everyone dug into their food. "Oh, this ham is delicious," Ferdinand said happily.

"You can thank Ryan for that," Stella said, "He's the one that prepared it."

"I didn't do that much," Ryan's cheeks turned red, "I just put the glaze on it and tossed it in the oven."

"Sounds like you did all the work to me," answered Stella's father.

"Did you put salt on these potatoes?" Dominic poked at his cheesy potatoes with a fork.

"I didn't put salt on anything," Stella said.

"That's a wise choice," Shelly handed the salt shaker to her husband. "You never know who might be watching their salt intake."

"Well, I'm not, that's for sure," Dominic said while he proceeded to sprinkle the salt on his potatoes and casserole.

"Me neither," added Celeste, "pass that salt shaker to me when you're done."

Everyone ate with contentment and complemented Stella and Ryan between bites. Roxanne took her post under the table, pawing at legs until someone surrendered a piece of ham or a glob of cheese. The plan worked well until she reached Stella.

"I think you have had quite enough," Stella leaned down to see two glowing eyes under the table. Roxanne retreated to the basement.

"You should be lucky she eats like she does," Celeste poked her fork into the casserole, "most people can't get their cats to eat."

"I know," Stella took a second helping of potatoes. "She just doesn't know when to stop. She's going to explode ones of these days."

"Yes, I know a certain someone who also doesn't know when to stop," Shelly glanced at her husband.

Dominic laughed and patted his round tummy. "Just more of me to love."

After lunch, Stella and Ryan cleared the table. Stella started filling the sink with soapy water while Ryan organized the dishes and put the leftover food back into the refrigerator.

Celeste and Shelly entered the kitchen, "Let us help you with that," Celeste said.

"Okay," Stella handed her mother a towel before turning to Ryan. "Why don't you and the guys divide up the presents while we work on the dishes."

Ryan kissed his wife on the cheek. "Can do."

Stella washed while Celeste dried and Shelly put the dishes back in their respected spots. Soon they were done and everything was cleaned up. They entered the living room to see all the presents were separated by recipient and Ryan was helping himself to more cookies.

Once everyone was seated by their gifts, the destruction began. Bows and ribbons were ripped off and thrown about. The sound of tearing paper filled the air and wrapping was scattered all over the floor. Roxanne reappeared from the basement to chase every discarded piece that moved, rolling with delight in the sea of paper, ribbon and bows. Stella was pleased that everyone loved the gifts she and Ryan had bought.

"Oh, that top is gorgeous," Shelly said, when her sister lifted out the blouse from its box.

"So is your handbag," Celeste pointed out.

"Yes, this will go with everything," Shelly examined the purse. "Thank you so much."

Ferdinand tried on his jacket, "I love it!"

"This cologne is great," Dominic opened the bottle and gave it a sniff. "I can't believe you found this. It's very hard to find."

Stella opened her gifts. Dominic and Shelly gave her a new apron to wear while she worked on her sculptures. It had all sorts of pockets to hold her tools. "This is wonderful, thank you so much." Her mother and father bought her a new clay gun and a year's subscription to her favorite sculpture magazine. "Thank you. I can't wait to use this gun," Stella read the packaging eagerly before turning to Ryan. "What did you get?"

She leaned in to see that Shelly and Dominic had given Ryan an expensive bottle of champagne. Celeste and Ferdinand gave him a new briefcase. "These are really great," Ryan addressed his guests. "Thank you very much."

"All right," Ferdinand reached for some of the wrapping. "Let's clean up this mess." As he grabbed the paper, Roxanne pounced on it, putting all her weight on it to keep him from picking it up.

"Sorry, girl," Ryan picked up the cat, "playtime is over."

"I'll go get a trash bag," Stella went into the kitchen and pulled out a trash bag from under the kitchen sink. All the wrapping paper and ribbons went into the bag, but Stella saved the bows to use another time. "Anyone care for more to drink?" Stella asked.

"I'll take another glass of wine," Dominic said.

"Oh, yes, me too," Celeste added.

"Make that three," Ferdinand said.

"I'm good," Shelly said with a smile.

Stella went back into the kitchen and soon appeared with a tray holding three wine glasses and two glasses of Pepsi for herself and Ryan. Even though Ryan didn't say anything, he never refused a glass of soda.

"Oh, thank you," Ryan took his glass. "How did you know?"

"ESP," Stella smiled. "Extra Spousal Perception." Everyone laughed.

The next few hours were spent catching up and talking. Celeste told her sister about receiving a lovely Christmas card from a distant aunt. Ryan, Ferdinand and Dominic discussed football and their predictions for the Super Bowl. Stella just sat back and enjoyed the conversations. Roxanne jumped into her lap and happily kneaded her pant leg. Stella's Christmas meal was a success, it was time to relax and enjoy time with her family.

In the late afternoon, Shelly turned to her husband. "We should get going. We have a long drive and I really want to get home before dark."

"Yes, that sounds like a good idea," Ferdinand stood and stretched. "It's hard to see that ice once the sun goes down."

Stella helped everyone pack up their gifts while Ryan returned to coat duty. As soon as all the guests were ready, they said goodbye.

"Everything was wonderful, dear," Celeste hugged Stella and kissed her goodbye.

"Yes, so glad you had us over," Shelly said.

"I'm glad you all could come," Stella hugged her aunt and uncle. "Everyone drive carefully on the way home."

"Enjoy your evening," Ferdinand kissed Stella. "Hope we didn't leave you with a mess."

Stella and Ryan watched from the window as the two cars pulled out of their driveway and left. Ryan excused himself, leaving Stella alone in the living room. She sat on the couch and decided on a cookie. Ryan returned with a grin on his face and a small package in his hand. It was wrapped in silver paper and topped with a deep purple bow.

"Merry Christmas," he said.

"Oh, how pretty," Stella kneeled by the Christmas tree and pulled out one of Ryan's presents as well the one from his stocking, "Merry Christmas."

They exchanged gifts. Stella opened hers slowly, for she wanted Ryan to open his first. Ryan opened the new CDs.

"All right. New music to listen to in the car." Then he opened his watch. "I love it," he kissed Stella.

"It's waterproof too," she said, "so you can't ruin it like you did the last one."

"Go on," Ryan said putting on his new watch. "Open yours."

Stella carefully removed the paper and saw it was a jewelry box. She grinned slyly at Ryan and then opened the box. Inside was a silver chain bracelet. Multi-colored gems were set along the whole chain in a rainbow fashion.

"Oh, it's so beautiful," Stella took out the bracelet with care. "Is it silver?"

"Platinum," Ryan helped Stella put the bracelet on her wrist. "Only the best for you."

Stella wrapped her arms around her husband and kissed him. "I love it and I love you."

"I love you too."

While Ryan cleaned up the mess and organized all the presents under the tree, Stella took the appetizers back into the kitchen and stored them in the refrigerator. Every so often, she would admire her bracelet; other than her engagement and wedding rings, this was the only other piece of jewelry Ryan had bought her. The colored gems brought back images of the Cave of Eternal Blaze. Its pastel crystals glimmered brightly, just like the precious stones on her wrist. Stella couldn't wait to go back to Mayazure to celebrate Christmas there. Ryan walked into the kitchen and opened the refrigerator.

"Making a leftover sandwich?" Stella asked.

"You know it," Ryan pulled out the plate of ham. "Want one?"

"Sure, why not?" Stella helped by taking out a couple of plates and placing a bun on each plate.

They took their food to the living room to watch television. No sooner had they sat down than Roxanne started begging at their feet. Stella slipped her a piece of ham while Ryan flipped through the channels. He settled on a classic Christmas movie and dug into his sandwich. Stella took a bite of hers as well. Though the ham was now cold, it was still delicious. Roxanne's attention was now on the glass of Stella's milk, which was sitting on the coffee table.

"You touch that milk and I'll skin your hide," Stella warned the cat. Ryan chuckled and sacrificed a piece of his own ham sandwich to Roxanne.

After they ate, Stella put the dishes in the sink and plopped back down on the couch next to her husband to finish watching the movie. Even Roxanne settled down and cuddled up in Ryan's lap. Stella couldn't help but feel at ease with her little family.

When the movie was over, Ryan stretched and yawned, "I don't know about you, but I'm exhausted."

Stella nodded. "I think there's nothing wrong with going to bed early."

Ryan offered to do cat-feeding duty while Stella went upstairs to get ready for bed. She removed her new bracelet and placed it in her jewelry box, where her grandmother's ring was waiting for her. She slipped the ring on just as Ryan entered the bedroom. Stella began removing her clothes to change into her pajamas, but Ryan had other plans. He walked over to his half-naked wife and put his arms around her.

"I don't think you need those tonight," Ryan nibbled at Stella's neck and she giggled.

"Is that so?" Stella asked. "How will I keep warm?"

"I'm sure we can find some way," Ryan said before kissing his wife passionately.

They fell into bed and made love. No thought of Mayazure, Jerot, Stella Cinereous or the upcoming battle crossed Stella's mind. The busy day with her parents and her aunt and uncle was wiped clean from Stella's memory. All she could think of was the pleasure she was feeling with her husband. After both were fulfilled from the lovemaking, they lay in bed and held each other. Stella played with Ryan's earlobe while he caressed her back.

"That seemed faster than usual," Ryan's breathing was heavy.

"We're tired," Stella murmured. "It was still good."

"That's all that matters," Ryan yawned as he pulled Stella closer. She laid her head against his chest and listened to his heartbeat. Before she knew it, she was gone from her world and back into another.

The Second Holiday

Stella arrived in the Welcome Garden and was greeted by Jerot, as usual. His Friesian and Radam, who was pacing nervously in the garden, accompanied him. Stella stepped off the round stone and gave Jerot a hug. She could feel his breath against her ear.

"Merry Christmas," she said.

"Merry Christmas to you," Jerot smiled as he looked at her.

Stella bent down and patted Radam on the head. "And to you too. Were you afraid I wasn't coming?"

"No, no," Radam squinted his eyes as he looked up at Stella.

"Liar," muttered Jerot. This made Stella giggle.

"You would too, if you had to be her guardian," Radam twitched his nose at the knight. "I worry every waking second she is gone."

"I am her guardian too," Jerot glared at the cat. "I have been with her longer than you and I worry just as much. I just don't show it." He pulled a red cloak off the horse's saddle and wrapped it around Stella. "Time's a-wasting," he said. "We'd better be off. Tuptup is preparing a special breakfast today."

"Oh, what is he making?" Stella asked, as Jerot helped her mount the Friesian.

"I don't know," Jerot picked up Radam and handed the cat to Stella. "He's been keeping it a secret."

Jerot took the reins of his horse and led the animal out of the garden and into the forest. Stella cradled Radam in her arms and he purred gently at her touch. As they came to the fork in the path, Stella looked up to see the vivid blue sky above. The early morning sun illuminated the snow to bright white, and the icicles on the trees glimmered like diamonds. Jerot continued to guide the horse through the forest. Stella spotted a small yellow bid, sitting on a tree branch, softly chirping a pleasant song. Radam licked his lips.

"That would make a yummy meal," he said.

Once they made it to the mountain and Jerot had stabled his horse, they climbed up the rock stairway to the cave. Stella was still carrying Radam in her arms and led the way, followed by Jerot.

"I could walk this on my own, you know," Radam protested.

"I thought you liked being held," Stella said.

"I do, but I'm not an invalid."

When they made it the entrance of the cave, Stella put Radam down to walk on his own, while Jerot lit a lantern. He took Stella's hand and the three of them entered the tunnel into the cavern. Stella couldn't help but enjoy holding Jerot's hand. It was firm, but soft, and put her at ease. They arrived at the cavern and Stella

was amazed at what she saw.
Streamers of red and green draped
along the ceiling of the cavern. Sprigs
of holly and mistletoe were scattered
about the streamers, and all the tents
had white banners, each with a
different Christmas image in red or
green. Jerot led Stella and Radam to
the Queen's tent. It was decorated
with a large wreath above the door.
Queen Iona was seated on her pillow
talking to Mullitor. Around the
dragon's neck was a large red bow
adorned with bells.

The Queen stood as Stella greeted
her. "Merry Christmas," said Stella as
she hugged her grandmother.

"Merry Christmas, dear," Queen
Iona kissed Stella on the cheek.

"Merry Christmas, Mullitor,"
Stella reached up and patted the
dragon on the nose. "You look very
festive."

"Why, thank you," Mullitor said.
"I rather like this bow."

"That reminds me," Queen Iona
reached by her pillow and pulled out a

smaller version of Mullitor's bow. "I made one for Radam as well."

"Oh no," Radam backed away. "I am not wearing that."

"Oh, yes you are," Jerot grabbed Radam and held him tight. Queen Iona fastened the bow around the cat's neck. Jerot let Radam go and he immediately tried to pull the bow off with his paws, with no luck.

"Rats," Radam pouted.

"I think it looks cute," Stella giggled. Radam shook his head to see if he could fling the bow off with force, but all it did was make the bells jingle. Tuptup emerged from the tent holding plates and silverware. He was wearing a red and white robe. He looked like a young, short Santa Claus.

"Merry Christmas," Stella said.

"Well, Merry Christmas to you," Tuptup said as he passed out the plates. "You arrived just in time. Breakfast is ready."

"Wonderful," Queen Iona beamed. "I don't know about the rest of you, but I'm starving."

"Same here," said Jerot.

Tuptup went back inside the tent and a few minutes later came back holding a large platter with a beautiful stollen. It was covered in a light glaze frosting and was steaming slightly.

"Oh, how magnificent," Queen Iona clasped her hands in joy. "It looks too pretty to eat."

"Can you cut this for me?" Tuptup handed a knife to Jerot. "I have some other things to prepare."

"Sure thing," Jerot sliced up the stollen and placed a piece on every plate. Tuptup returned with jars of jam and a small bowl of butter.

"I like a little jam and butter on my stollen," he said, "and I'm willing to share if anyone else would like to try it."

"I think I would like to try the jam," said Stella. "Sounds good." Stella spread strawberry jam on her slice. Even Mullitor and Radam had some stollen.

Stella bit into it and instantly tasted sweet fruit and salty nuts in the cake. The jam added moisture and

Stella closed her eyes, savoring the flavor.

"This is exceptionally exquisite," Queen Iona said. "I think another slice will be in order."

"Yes," Mullitor added. "The sweetness is heavenly."

Tuptup sliced second helpings for everyone except Radam, who was still picking at his first piece.

"Do you not like it?" Stella asked the cat.

"It's okay," Radam said. "I'm just not a fruit and nut kind of cat." He looked at Tuptup, "No offense, of course, to your fine cooking."

"None taken," Tuptup said. "Perhaps I have something more to your liking," and he slipped back into the tent. He returned holding a small bowl in his hands. "Here is some leftover tuna. I'm sure this will be better."

"Oh, yes. Thank you," Radam said, before burying his head into the bowl.

"I will take that stollen off your hands," Mullitor said to the cat, and helped himself.

Once everyone was full and the stollen was gone, Stella and Jerot volunteered to clear the dishes. The Minots went to work washing the dishes, using as little water as possible from the canteens. Stella and Jerot helped with drying the dishes and Jerot hummed a simple tune while he worked. Otherwise, he seemed very quiet. Stella wondered if he was thinking about past holidays with his wife. Stella decided not to pry. Finally, Jerot spoke.

"The children are going to visit 'Santa' this morning. Would you like to watch?"

"Oh, yes," Stella smiled. "Who's playing Santa this year?" She distinctively remembered when Jerot was almost drafted for the position.

"George Bylane is doing it this year," Jerot said as he put the final dishes away. "He teaches the seven-and eight-year old children."

"Oh, he sounds perfect," Stella watched the Minots drain the sink.

"He's a little too skinny, but that can be fixed," Jerot said. They left the tent to find the Queen sitting on her pillow, knitting a green hat. Tuptup was laughing at poor Radam, who was still trying to get rid of his bow.

"We're going to watch the children talk to Santa," Stella said to her grandmother. "Want to join us?"

"Absolutely," Queen Iona put down her knitting. "In fact, I have a few things to ask Santa for this year," she winked.

The group of six went deeper into the cavern, where they found the line of children beginning to form. Some were in line with a parent, but the older children braved their visit alone while their parents stood off to the side and watched. At the head of the line was a large wooden chair. The Queen took her place at the other end of the line.

"This is exciting," she said. "Come Stella, stand in line with me."

"Oh, okay," Stella was hesitant. She was a little too old for Santa, "but only because I have to keep an eye on you." Queen Iona giggled. Three women stepped forward.

"Is everyone ready for Santa?" one of the women called out.

All the children cheered. The Queen clapped her hands with elation. Stella felt awkward, in line with all these children, but seeing the bright, happy face of her grandmother made her smile. She ignored the others, standing off to the side, who snickered at them.

"All right," the woman continued, "here's Santa."

Out popped George from a corner nook, wearing a bright red velvet robe trimmed with fluffy cotton. A large pillow was stuffed down his front and more cotton was fashioned into a wig and beard. His entire outfit was topped with a matching red velvet beret, also trimmed with cotton. The children applauded at the sight of him.

"Oh, isn't he wonderful?" Queen Iona asked Stella. "He looks perfect."

"Ho! Ho! Ho!" bellowed George. He took his seat at the wooden chair and the first child walked up to sit on his lap. The little girl with blonde pigtails was wearing a festive green dress. In her arms was a stuffed bunny rabbit, wearing a blue dress. "Well, hello there little girl. What is your name?" As if George didn't already know.

"Vanessa," the little girl answered.

"Well, Vanessa," George pinched her cheek and she giggled with delight, "tell Santa what you would like for Christmas."

Vanessa looked over at her parents. They smiled and waved at her, giving her encouragement. "Well," she said as she picked at the hem of her dress, "what I really want is to go home."

The whole cavern went silent. Vanessa's mother lowered her head in embarrassment. How would George handle this simple, but complicated, wish?

"Hmm," George stroked his fake beard, "that seems to be something Santa can't handle, but I know someone who can." He pointed to the Queen. "Queen Iona is the one you should be asking."

"Don't you worry dear," Queen Iona waved to get Vanessa's attention. "In no time, we will all be going home." Vanessa smiled and seemed pleased with the Queen's answer.

"Now," George continued, "is there anything else that I might be able to get for you?"

Vanessa nodded and held up her stuffed bunny rabbit, "I would like a new dress for Bun-Bun," she said.

"Now *that* I can do," George said, and Vanessa hopped off his lap.

The line moved along steadily as the children took turns on Santa's lap. Most of the children wanted toys. Some of the older children asked for more practical things, like a new bridle for their horse or their very own practice sword. After standing in line for two hours, it was finally the Queen's turn.

"Ho! Ho! Ho!" George said as the Queen took her place on his lap. "Tell me what you would like, little girl."

Queen Iona giggled with amusement, "I need a new pair of dress shoes," she lifted up her gown slightly to reveal the worn shoes on her feet. "These babies are starting to wear thin."

"Anything else?" asked George.

The Queen thought for a moment, "Yes," she answered. "I would like a new corset. I think that will do."

"All right, I'll see what I can do," and Queen Iona jumped off George's lap.

"Well, that was fun," Stella said as she went to escort her grandmother away from the line.

"Oh, we're not done," Queen Iona smiled. "It's your turn to sit on Santa's lap."

"Oh, I don't know," Stella could feel her cheeks blush, but then she remembered all the years when her grandmother would take her to the mall to see Santa. Stella was no longer a little girl, but it felt right to join in on the fun. "Okay, but only for you," she said. She carefully sat on George's lap as he roared out another string of ho ho ho's.

"And what would you like, little girl?" George winked at Stella.

Stella sighed. She had no idea what she wanted. Anything she asked for would just be in vain. She wasn't really going to get anything. Stella glanced up to see her friends and her grandmother, watching and waiting. Her eyes caught Jerot's face and an idea popped in her head; something her grandmother had said earlier. Stella knew she wasn't going to get it, but it was a good thing to ask for.

"I would like my own bow and quiver," she said.

"Ho! Ho! Ho! That sounds like a reasonable gift," George again stroked his fake beard. "Anything else?"

"No, I think that's good."

"Splendid. I'll work on that right away," George said as Stella stood up. All she really wanted was to get off his lap. She joined the rest of the group, who all had grins on their faces. Stella felt awkward.

"So, a bow and quiver," Jerot mused as they walked back to the Queen's tent. "That sounds like a great gift, for any up and coming archer."

"Well, I'm going to need something for next week," Stella said, "with the battle and all."

"Well, you can always borrow one from the supply tent," said Queen Iona.

"Yes, yes," Jerot rubbed his chin much like George had done. "That is an option."

Back at the tent, Tuptup excused himself to prepare lunch. The Queen, Jerot and Stella sat down on their pillows around the fire and Radam took up space on Stella's lap, where he happily decided to take a nap.

"Do you need any help?" Stella said.

"Nope, it's going to be a simple lunch," Tuptup said as headed for the tent. "The big meal will be dinner."

"Well, you just call out if you need it," Queen Iona said, picking up her half-completed green hat.

"I should go on the hunt for lunch." Mullitor said.

"Be careful out there," Stella said. Mullitor lowered his head and she gave him a gentle pat on the snout before he departed.

"Wanna play some Givlok?" Jerot pulled out a deck of cards.

Stella wrinkled her nose. She was no good at the game, but there was really nothing else to do. "I suppose so."

"Great," and Jerot shuffled the cards.

Several minutes passed and already Stella began to get frustrated with the game. Radam would open an eye to glance at her cards and he whispered hints to her, but Stella still couldn't remember all the complicated rules. After a few minutes of aggravation, Tuptup called out for assistance.

"I'm on it," Stella put down her cards and moved Radam from her lap.

She was glad to do anything to stop playing Givlok. She entered the tent to see Tuptup had prepared a tray of Sloppy Joes. He handed Stella a stack of plates.

"Take these and the tray out," he said, "and take drink orders for me, while I get out these glasses."

"No problem," Stella balanced the tray in one hand and the plates in another.

"Oh, Sloppy Joes," Jerot put his deck of cards away. "My favorite."

"Everything is your favorite," Queen Iona put down her knitting and took a plate.

"What would everyone like to drink?" Stella asked. She carefully took apart a Sloppy Joe and just put the meat on a plate for Radam.

"I'll have some ale," Jerot grabbed two sandwiches off the tray.

"Milk, please," said Queen Iona, "cow, of course," she added with a wink.

"Milk for me too," said Radam.

"Okay. Be right back," Stella went back into the tent. "Two milks and two ales, please." Stella felt adventurous and decided to try what Jerot was having.

"Alright," Tuptup took the bottle of ale and began to pour. "Go make yourself comfortable and I'll be right out."

Stella made her way back to her pillow and took a Sloppy Joe off the tray for herself. The bun was soft and the meat was tender and juicy. Everyone chewed with delight as Tuptup brought out the drinks. Stella tried the ale; it was … interesting. Not at all like beer, but more bitter, like vinegar. She tried her best to drink it all.

"How's the ale?" Queen Iona asked.

"It's different," Stella said, "definitely unlike anything we have on Earth." Her grandmother smiled.

After lunch, Stella rubbed Radam's full stomach as he purred with glee. The Queen returned to her knitting, humming a tune.

"Who's the hat for?" Stella asked.

"Oh, no one in particular," Queen Iona said. "I've never made a hat before and thought I should try it."

"Well, it looks like you're doing a good job," said Radam.

"You think so?" Queen Iona held up her work. "I can't really tell when it's only half done."

"I'm sure it will be wonderful," Stella said.

Mullitor returned, feeling sluggish. He made his way to the tent and collapsed in a heap to take a nap.

"Everything okay?" asked Stella.

"Oh yes," the dragon said. "I just got greedy and ate way too much."

"I hope you saved some of the birds for me," chuckled Radam.

"Of course he has," Queen Iona reached over and rubbed the cat's tummy. "I don't think Mullitor is that huge of a pig."

"Not at all," Mullitor answered and closed his eyes.

Tuptup and Jerot emerged from the tent. Jerot was holding a large sack slung over his shoulders.

"Time for presents!" Jerot said joyfully.

"Oh, goody," Queen Iona set down her knitting and clasped her hands with delight. Jerot opened the sack and Tuptup passed out the gifts. Everyone got a present, even Stella. She looked at the small square box wrapped in simple brown paper, adorned with a red bow. A small tag read *Stella*, but didn't say whom it was from.

"Who is this from?" she asked.

"Why, Santa Claus, of course," said Tuptup.

Stella looked back at her gift. Surely Santa wasn't real … at least, he wasn't real on Earth. She decided not to worry about it and opened her present. She ripped off the bow and paper and lifted the lid. Inside was a coiled belt made of fine leather. Stella took it out of the box. The buckle was made of silver and adorned with sapphires. It was quite beautiful.

"Oh, how pretty," Queen Iona saw Stella's gift. "Try it on."

Stella put on the belt, pulling it through the belt loops of her jeans. She fastened the buckle and modeled the belt for everyone to see.

"Very nice," Mullitor said.

"Yes, it goes quite well with your sweater," Jerot smiled.

Everyone else opened their gifts while Stella helped Radam open his. The Queen received her new shoes and corset that she had requested when she was on George's lap. Jerot received a plum-colored doublet that fit quite nicely. Tuptup opened a new ink and quill set. Mullitor received a large chunk of venison and Radam received a collar that matched Stella's belt. It was made of silver and had sapphires set into it.

"That is gorgeous," Tuptup examined the collar.

"Yes, much better than this stupid bow," Radam pawed at the red bow still tied around his neck. Stella giggled and helped Radam to replace it with the collar.

"It looks very nice on you," said Queen Iona as she put on her new shoes.

Radam looked at his reflection in a clear crystal on the cavern floor. "This is something I should only wear on special occasions," he said.

"Well, today is a special occasion, so wear it," Stella patted the cat on the head.

Stella helped Tuptup clear up all the wrappings before settling down by the fire. Mullitor went back to his nap, while the Queen decided to check on her people and find out what they got from Santa. Radam played with a leftover strand of ribbon.

"Care to play more Givlok?" Jerot asked Stella.

"Let's play a game I know," Stella said. "Let's play Gin Rummy. Tuptup, would you care to join us?"

"Absolutely," Tuptup pulled up his pillow next to Jerot. "What kind of game is it?"

"It's like Givlok, but easier."

"Sounds like my type of game," Tuptup rubbed his hands together.

Stella divided up the cards and taught the rules to Jerot and Tuptup. After an hour, Stella had won most of the games, but let Jerot and Tuptup each win once just to make them happy. The Queen returned, looking very pleased.

"Did everyone get what they wanted this year?" Jerot asked her as he scanned over his cards.

"Oh yes, everyone seems to be so happy," Queen Iona smiled. "The children are going outside to play in the snow and I think I will join them. Who else wants to go?"

"Oh, I do," Stella said, tired of being cooped up indoors.

"I do too," Jerot put down his cards. Stella saw he had a lousy hand. "What do you say, Tuptup?"

"Ah, I think I will join you as well," said the dwarf, "as long as we keep the snowball fights to a minimum." Everyone laughed.

The Queen, Stella, Jerot, and Tuptup wrapped themselves up in cloaks, mittens and hats. Radam felt left out.

"I should make you a sweater," Queen Iona said to the cat, "then you wouldn't have to be so cold."

"I'll be all right," Radam said, letting Stella pick him up. "I have my fur to keep me warm."

The group tip-toed past the sleeping dragon with Jerot at the lead, holding a lantern. When they made it to the cave entrance, Stella looked down to see several children already playing in the snow. Some were making snow forts to prepare for a snowball battle, while others were practicing their snow angel techniques.

"Oh, I love snow angels," Stella passed Radam to her grandmother and ran out to join the children. She flopped over on her back. Stella waved her arms and moved her legs back and forth before finally standing up. The result was a large angel in among the group of smaller ones.

"It's perfect," said Jerot with a smile.

"I agree," said Queen Iona.

"Thank you," Stella felt her cheeks blush, as Jerot looked at her longingly.

For several hours, they played in the snow with the children. Tuptup and Jerot joined the snow fort battle, each picking a side, while Stella and her grandmother helped the children make a snowman. Radam pounced and pranced in the snow until little clumps of ice collected in his fur. More snow fell in large flakes and Stella taught the children how to catch them on their tongues. She laughed with delight at the sight of the children running around with their tongues sticking out, almost running into each other. After a while, Jerot join Stella and the Queen; he was covered in snow.

"Did you win?" Stella helped brush the snow off Jerot's back.

"You bet I did," Jerot shook the snow off his boot. "Now I'm hungry again from all the fun."

The Queen looked up at the sky, "It is getting close to dinner time," she said.

Tuptup joined them. He too was covered in snow, and he had clusters of snow in his beard. "Aye, I should start on the food." Once they found Radam, they returned to the cave and brought the children back to their parents.

Then they sat around the fire warming themselves with cups of hot chocolate. Mullitor had awakened and let Stella huddle up against his side. His soft skin felt like a giant fleece blanket. Radam took comfort in Stella's lap. He purred softly; he was in a total state of relaxation. Tuptup called out for help, so Jerot entered the tent.

"What are we having anyway?" asked Stella.

"Jerot caught a large turkey the other day," Queen Iona said.

"Turkey?" Radam's ears perked up at the word. "Now that I can eat."

"I hope there's enough for me," Mullitor said.

"Of course," said Queen Iona, "It is a rather large bird."

Tuptup and Jerot emerged from the tent together holding a gigantic tray. On it was a bird so big, Stella was sure it was an ostrich and not a turkey.

Surrounding the turkey were carrots, potatoes and small ears of corn.

"Are you sure that was a turkey?" Stella asked, as Jerot and Tuptup set it down by the fire.

"Looks like a turkey to me," Radam licked his lips.

"Sure was," said Jerot. "Biggest thing I have ever seen. Took three arrows to take him down."

Plates were passed out while Tuptup carved the massive bird. Mullitor was given one leg while the other was saved for Jerot. Stella was offered a wing, but passed it up for a smaller slice of breast. She also took a few potatoes and carrots and an ear of corn. Stella bit into the turkey and it was the juiciest thing she had ever tasted. The rich flavor melted in her mouth and the texture was not chewy at all.

"Does anyone need gravy?" Tuptup went to get up.

"None for me," Queen Iona chewed on a piece of carrot. "Everything is just scrumptious."

"Yeah, it's really wonderful," said Stella.

"I wouldn't mind a little gravy," said Jerot as he ripped off a piece of the leg.

"I would like to try some too," said Mullitor.

Tuptup went into the tent and brought back a small bowl filled with a light brown gravy. He helped pour some onto Mullitor's turkey leg before letting Jerot help himself.

After dinner, Stella helped the Minots with the dishes while Tuptup packed the rest of the turkey away for later.

"Are you sure you're done?" Tuptup asked. "You didn't eat that much."

Stella felt so full that the idea of having more sickened her. "No, that's okay," she said. "I'm good for a while."

"Well, you know where it is if you change your mind."

After dinner, they all relaxed by the fire.

"Tuptup, dear," Queen Iona said, "why don't you bring out that guitar so we can sing some Christmas carols."

"That sounds like a great idea," Radam said. Mullitor nodded his head in agreement.

"I hope you don't mind," Stella said as Tuptup went back into the tent, "but I think I'm going to take a walk. I need to burn off some of this food."

"You do that," said Queen Iona, "and when you come back, you can join us."

"I should go with you," said Radam.

"No, that won't be necessary," Stella said. "I'm not going far."

Radam's ears laid flat against his head, "Are you sure?"

"Don't worry so much," Queen Iona smiled at the cat.

Stella went to the tunnel and took a lantern to lead her way. The sun had set and stars had begun to appear in the sky. She sat at the ledge of the cave entrance to meditate and think.

Stella remembered the first time she had come to the cave and met Mullitor. She remembered introducing him to the sound of laughter, and he introduced her to the cavern. Stella took a deep breath and slowly exhaled. She looked over to the distant city of Cobalian. The image made her angry; she wished she could wring that blonde witch's neck.

"You look awfully lonely" Stella turned, a little disappointed to see Jerot had followed her. "May I join you?"

Stella looked back out into the forest and folded her arms. "I guess you may, since you're here."

Jerot set his lantern next to Stella's and sat down beside her. For a few minutes, they were silent, simply watching the night.

"I got you something," Jerot held out a box he was carrying. It was wrapped in white paper with a purple bow.

"Jerot, you didn't have to get me a gift," Stella said, embarrassed. "You know I couldn't get you anything."

"I know, but this is something you need."

"Well, it is wrapped nicely," Stella took the box and opened it. Inside was a brand-new bow made of yew wood and accented with gold. "Oh my," she took the bow out of the box and saw etched in gold were the words *For Stella*. Under the bow was a quiver in light tan leather also trimmed with gold.

"Remember when I went to Wreckton and I had the Queen pay me six hundred gold instead of seven hundred?" Jerot asked.

"Yes, I do remember," Stella ran her hand along the bow. It was smooth to the touch. "You mean you spent two hundred gold on this?"

"No price is too high for you."

Stella felt a twinge of guilt. "But I got you nothing."

"You being here is the best gift for me," Jerot said.

"Will you take care of this when I'm not here?" Stella carefully placed the bow back in the box atop the quiver.

"Of course," Jerot smiled. He stood up and helped Stella to her feet. They looked at one another and again, Stella felt the urge to kiss him.

"We should go back," Stella said, abruptly. "I'm getting a little cold."

"There's just one more thing," Jerot pointed up and Stella looked. There, on the ceiling of the cave above them, was a small sprig of mistletoe. Stella's eyes grew wide in surprise at the tiny greenery with the white berries looking down upon them. She looked back at Jerot; she knew she had been tricked.

"It's just a plant, you know," she said.

"True, but it's tradition," Jerot couldn't help but smile.

Stella closed her eyes and took a deep breath. She rubbed her left arm as a reflex. She did want to kiss him so much, but still, it was wrong. Finally, she spoke.

"Okay, maybe just a little kiss, for tradition's sake," she said. "But if you tell anyone -"

Stella didn't finish her sentence. Jerot pulled her to him and kissed her passionately. Euphoria rushed through Stella. *Oh God, I want this man*, she thought. The bow and quiver slipped out of Stella's hands and fell to the floor. Her arms wrapped around Jerot's neck as his hands roamed underneath her sweater, caressing her back. Stella grabbed Jerot's hair; she liked tugging at it. He kissed her neck as he fumbled, trying to unhook her bra. Stella nibbled at his ear; her breathing began to get deeper. *No, no, no. You can't do this. Think about what you are doing to Ryan.*

The thought of her husband snapped Stella out of the spell. "Stop," she whispered into Jerot's ear, but he wasn't listening. "Stop," she said a little louder. Jerot looked at her and went to kiss her again, but she pushed him away. "No," was all she said.

"I can't help but think you like it as much as I do," Jerot whispered. "Admit it."

"The only thing I will admit is that I was thinking of Ryan when you kissed me," said Stella. Those words stung Jerot in his heart. He closed his eyes as if he were in pain. Stella managed to get out of his grip and reached down to pick up the bow. "I'm very cold," she said.

"Indeed you are," Jerot answered.

"We should go back," Stella grabbed her lantern. Jerot did the same. Their trip through the tunnel was silent. Stella could hear Jerot breathing behind her. She felt so horrible to treat Jerot so harshly, but she couldn't love him. Jerot had to understand.

They made it back to the Queen's tent. "Look what Jerot gave me," Stella showed her grandmother the bow and quiver inside the box. Jerot grinned at the thought of Stella appreciating his gift, but he was still hurt inside.

"How pretty," said Queen Iona. "Looks like Santa got you what you wanted." Stella had asked 'Santa' for a bow and quiver. Jerot knew her better than she thought.

The rest of the evening was filled with caroling. Jerot went to his tent to get his guitar and he and Tuptup played while the others sang. Jerot strummed cords while Tuptup played the melodies. Stella didn't know any of the songs, so she clapped along to the rhythm.

When it got late, the Queen and Tuptup retired to their tent, while Mullitor and Radam cuddled up together in a corner, keeping each other warm. Stella and Jerot were alone once again. She felt a sense of awkwardness as she stared into the low burning fire. Stella tried not to look, but she knew Jerot was watching her. Finally, she spoke.

"I never got to properly thank you for your present, so, thank you."

Jerot scooted up next to her. "I know and you're welcome."

"I'm very sorry about earlier," Stella still looked into the fire. "I didn't mean to hurt your feelings."

"It's quite okay," Jerot picked up a twig and starting poking at the embers. "You were just being honest."

Stella hadn't lied about thinking of Ryan. Jerot wrapped an arm around Stella's shoulders. She look up at him and met his vivid blue eyes. The urge to kiss him returned. She had to stop herself.

"It is getting late," Stella said. "I should prepare myself to start practicing for battle when I come back tomorrow."

"Atta girl," Jerot smiled. "I bet that bow will be much easier to use. It's very light." He leaned in and kissed Stella on the forehead. "Merry Christmas."

"You too," Stella got up and went into the tent.

Inside, Tuptup was fast asleep, but the Queen was still awake, lying on her cot. "Coming to bed so soon?" she asked Stella.

"I am kind of tired," Stella said as she changed into her nightgown. "I must physically and mentally prepare myself for battle, starting tomorrow."

"Good idea," Queen Iona grinned. "Did you have a good Christmas?"

Stella smiled. She had never expected to spend another holiday with her grandmother. As she hopped into bed she said, "Grandma, this was the best Christmas ever."

The Battle

Soon, the day of the battle arrived. Stella was as prepared as she could be. The new bow and quiver were perfect. The bow's size and weight made it easy for Stella to aim, and she was shooting the best she ever had. Jerot had taken her out into the forest to hunt. Stella killed her first deer and a vulture. She donated the venison to some of the Cobalian people and the vulture was taken care of by Mullitor.

Jerot even took Stella to Wreckton to get more supplies. The goblin city was alive with engineering wonders and tiny green people, smaller than Tuptup. They had long pointy ears and some even had long noses. They were friendly people, and helped get everything that Jerot and Stella needed. Jerot bought Stella a set of armor made of thick leather to wear in battle, even though Stella tried to convince him otherwise.

Stella arrived at the Welcome Garden where Jerot and Radam were waiting. There was a somber heaviness to the air. The joyous times were over and the serious times had begun.

"We have a busy day ahead of us," Jerot said as he wrapped Stella in a cloak. "I want to get some archery practice in before we go to Chamoisee Canyon, and I need to adjust your armor. The shoulders are too big."

"That sounds fine," Stella hopped onto Jerot's horse. "But can we first have breakfast?"

"Yes, you can't win a battle without food," said Radam as Jerot hoisted him up and placed him in Stella's arms."

Jerot smiled, "Of course we are going to have breakfast. I never miss a meal."

"It's starting to show," Radam said. "Your tunic looks a little tight."

Stella giggled as Jerot fought to adjust his tunic. He led his Friesian out of the garden and into the forest. The sky was covered in dark gray clouds that looked more like smoke. No birds were singing, and there was no sign of forest creatures.

Stella looked to the sky, "I hope it doesn't snow."

"The canyon hardly gets any snow," said Jerot. "We don't have to worry about it."

"But we still have to travel to get there. I don't know about you, but I don't feel like trudging through a bunch of snow."

"Don't be such a baby. It's just frozen rain."

They made it to the cave and went inside. The cavern was busy with people either fixing their armor or practicing their fighting techniques. Stella was used to this; they had been busy since the day after Christmas. The Queen was sitting by the fire, holding a piece of parchment and showing it to Mullitor.

"What do you have there?" Stella sat next to her grandmother.

"Battle plans," Queen Iona said. She showed Stella the parchment. A dark black line was drawn down the center of the paper. One side of the line had red dots the other side had blue. Arrows pointing from the blue indicated the directions they were going. "We are the blue dots," she pointed on the map. "We will be on the south cliff, west of this line. The line is the Battle Line. It is where the two parties will meet."

"Oh," Stella nodded, "kind of like the line of scrimmage in football."

"What?" Mullitor seemed confused.

"Nevermind."

The Queen rolled up the parchment and put it aside as Tuptup appeared from the tent with plates. "Hope everyone is hungry," he said, passing out the plates. "I made a large stack of pancakes this morning."

"I'm famished," Jerot took his plate.

"Good," Tuptup went back into the tent and brought out a large platter of pancakes, a small tub of butter and a pitcher of maple syrup. He also brought out two bowls of left over turkey from Christmas, for Mullitor and Radam.

Stella took three pancakes and applied butter to them. She wasn't a fan of syrup. The Queen and Tuptup also took a few pancakes, but Jerot piled ten on his plate. The Queen simply shook her head in frustration. Everyone ate in silence; the upcoming battle was a heavy weight on all of them. Finally Mullitor spoke.

"After breakfast, should I fly over Cobalian and report anything I find?"

"No, my friend," Queen Iona said. "They will be expecting you, and might try to shoot you down."

"Please," Mullitor nudged the Queen on the shoulder. "If you couldn't do it, I doubt they can."

Tuptup roared with laughter that echoed through the cavern. It filled the silence with a sense of awkwardness. The others gave him a strange look.

"Well, I thought it was funny," he said.

"Indeed," said Queen Iona with a smile. "Thank you for that cheerful sound." She looked at Mullitor. "If you feel it is safe, then by all means go. Just be careful."

After breakfast, Stella offered to help Tuptup clear the dishes. "It's quite all right," he said. "You have more important things to do."

"Yes, she does," Jerot stood up and stretched. "You should practice your archery while I resize that armor."

"Don't press her too hard," Queen Iona went back to her piece of parchment, "or she will fail us in battle."

"I wouldn't dare fail you," Stella said.

"As long as you stay with the other archers, you won't," said Radam. "Remember what Mistis said."

"I know, I know," Stella sighed. She took Jerot by the arm, "Come on, let's get to work."

Stella, Jerot and Radam went to Jerot's tent in the back of the cavern. Jerot had acquired new sacks of grain for Stella to shoot at. As Stella set herself up for target practice, Jerot pulled the leather armor from his tent, as well as a sharp hunting knife.

"I'm not too good at this leatherworking," he said, "so forgive me if it's a bit rough."

"As long as it protects me," Stella raised her bow and took aim at the sack to the right. Since her new bow was so light, Stella had no need to slouch her elbow. This gave her the perfect opportunity to work on her breathing. She let go of the arrow and it sailed just left of the bull's eye. Stella was pleased. After an hour, Jerot called her over to test out the armor.

"How you doing so far?" he asked.

"Good," Stella put down her bow. "Nothing farther than an inch from the bull's eye."

"That *is* good," Jerot helped Stella into her armor. It consisted of a helmet, shoulder guards, a chest piece and arm and leg guards. The leather was light enough that Stella didn't feel awkward. "How does it fit?"

"Okay," Stella adjusted the chest piece.

"Looks good to me," said Radam.

"Why don't you shoot a couple of arrows with it on and let me see if everything looks all right," Jerot said.

Stella nodded and picked up her bow. She pulled an arrow out of her quiver, took aim and fired. She shot a few more just for good measure.

"This arm guard is a little too long," she gestured her right arm. "I'm having trouble bending it when I pull the arrow back."

"Give it here and I'll see what I can do," Jerot said.

Stella practiced a while longer, but soon grew tired. She needed to save her energy for the battle. Stella sat on the floor next to Jerot while he worked on her arm guard.

"Getting tired?" Jerot looked up at Stella.

"Yeah, I think I need a break." Stella removed her helmet. Radam took comfort in her lap.

"That's fine," Jerot went back to work. "You are doing exceptionally well. I see no reason to make you do more." Once finished with the arm guard, Stella put it back on and shot a few more arrows to test it.

"It's perfect," she said.

"Good to hear," Jerot helped Stella out of the armor. "Now let's go register with the Battle Keeper."

"Who?" Radam asked. Stella also wasn't sure who that was.

"The Battle Keeper," Jerot explained. "He takes the name and physical description of everyone who goes into battle. That way," Jerot awkwardly scratched his head, "we can identify bodies if we need to."

"Oh dear," Radam pawed the floor nervously.

"There is nothing to fear," Jerot reassured the cat. "You know that archers rarely die in battle."

They headed to the main area of the cavern, where Stella saw a large crowd of people gathered in the place where George had played Santa earlier. It was no longer a joyous gathering. The crowd surrounded an old man who had a long graying beard that reached to his knees.   He was dressed in fine silver robes, and in his hands were a quill and a long piece of parchment that fell to the floor and rolled behind him.

"That is Adraham," said Jerot, "He is the official Battle Keeper."

"Well, let's get this over with," Stella said. She didn't want to admit she was slightly scared. It was the first time that she had thought of the possibility of dying in battle. What would happen if she died in Mayazure? Would she never get home, or would she be sent home never to return? Stella thought it best not to ask Jerot. The three joined the crowd and soon it was their turn to talk to Adraham.

"Well, hello there, Jerot," the old man smiled. He quickly wrote down Jerot's name on the parchment. "Participating in the battle today?"

"Of course," Jerot answered. Adraham continued to write.

"And will you be wearing your standard tabard?"

"Yes," Jerot spoke, "blue with a white heart topped with a gold crown."

"Excellent," Adraham finished writing and then look down at Stella. "I'm afraid I don't know you, young lady."

"I am Stella Tyrian," Stella spoke as Adraham wrote, "that's T-Y-R-I-A-N"

"Yes, yes," Adraham muttered while writing down Stella's physical description. "Young lady, long brown hair, slim goggles."

"They're called glasses," Stella corrected him.

"Ah, thank you. What weapon are you using today?"

"My bow. It is made of yew and has my name engraved on it. I will also be wearing leather armor that has been modified on the shoulders and right arm."

"Good, good," Adraham scribbled this all down, "Thank you. I think that is enough."

"Don't forget me," Radam pawed at Adraham's robes.

"You're not fighting in the battle," Jerot raised an eyebrow.

"No, but I will be there," the cat turned toward the Battle Keeper. "My name is Radam."

"Very good," Adraham wrote some more, "Orange-colored feline, domestic size. Yes, that should be good."

"Thank you," Radam seemed pleased with himself.

"Well, let's head to the Queen's tent," Jerot said. "It's nearly lunch time and I'm starving."

"Yes, I am feeling a little hungry too," Stella said. They made their way out of the crowd and towards the Queen's tent, where she was busy polishing a set of plate armor decorated in blue enamel and silver.

"What have you got there?" Radam stared at his reflection in a piece of the armor.

"This is my armor," Queen Iona said. "Did you think I would sit here and hide, while my people fought for their city?"

"Of course not," Radam said. "I just didn't think you would be fighting."

"I'm not planning on it, but you never know."

"Any word on what's for lunch?" Stella changed the subject.

"I believe we are having lasagna," Queen Iona put down the last piece of armor. "It will be filling and last us through the battle."

"Great," Jerot took a seat by the fire. "I could go for some pasta."

Tuptup soon appeared with plates and a large pan full of lasagna. Everyone took a piece and it was indeed filling. Stella was full after the first piece. While they ate, Mullitor had returned from his own lunch.

"Any news from the enemy?" Jerot helped himself to a second piece.

"Yes, they are already beginning to take formation," Mullitor said. "I would predict that they would be on the move to the canyon within the hour."

"Then we will prepare as well," Queen Iona handed her empty plate to Tuptup. "Everyone finish what is on your plate. We must take to the battleground. The Minots can handle the dishes on their own, Tuptup."

"But I'm still hungry," Jerot whined.

"Tough." Queen Iona stood up and turned toward the people, who adored her. "My friends, it is time to set up formation for battle. The trek is long and we must leave quickly." Her voice echoed across the cavern. Stella had never heard her grandmother speak in such a strong tone. "All knights in front, ten people to a line. Behind them, all warriors with melee weapons, ten people to a line. Behind them, all archers will assemble, also at ten to a line. The best archers shall be at the front, followed in order by those with descending skill. The formation will be constructed at the foot of this mountain."

With these words, the people moved, putting on their armor, grabbing their weapons and filing out of the cavern. Hardly anyone spoke.

"Come on," Jerot whispered to Stella. "We need to get into our armor." He led Stella back to his tent, and Radam followed. Jerot helped Stella into her armor before putting on his own. Jerot placed his sword around his waist, while Stella pulled her hair into a ponytail, slung her quiver onto her back and picked up her bow. Within minutes, they were ready. They headed back to the Queen's tent. The Queen was in her plate armor, and Tuptup was in his own leather armor. It had a tint of green, and he was holding Adraham's rolled up parchment. The cavern was almost completely empty.

"Are we ready?" Queen Iona looked at her friends. Stella and the others nodded. The Queen turned to Mullitor. "Dear, I want you to fly above the battle at all times. Once both parties are ready, I want you to let out a roar to signal the start of battle. Under no circumstances should you aid in battle. That would be unfair."

"As you wish," Mullitor replied.

"Then let us go."

The six walked through the tunnel led by Mullitor. When they reached the foot of the mountain, Stella saw that everyone was in formation. As Mullitor took flight and flew on ahead, Tuptup went to the stable to fetch the Queen's white Arabian. She mounted her horse and turned to Jerot.

"You and Stella go into formation," she said. "Put Stella in with the archers where you think she should go."

"Will do," Jerot took hold of Stella's hand. His hand was slightly sweaty. Radam followed Stella closely. They walked along the side of the formation to the first line of the archers. "You are quite good, so I think you should be in front."

"I should?" Stella asked nervously.

"Don't you worry. The ones with the melee weapons will protect you. All you have to do is shoot arrows." He kissed Stella on the cheek and went up to the front with the other knights. Stella and Radam took their place in formation and the other archers shifted to accommodate them.

Stella stood between two men. The man on her left was an older man in his late fifties, with a short gray beard and broad shoulders. The man on her right was younger, about her age. He had hair of gold and was built strongly. The old man greeted Stella and Radam.

"Hello, I'm Ristopher," he pointed to the man on her right, "and that is my son Tenjamin." Ristopher's son nodded to Stella.

"I'm Stella and this is Radam. It is nice to meet you."

"Are you a friend of Jerot?" Tenjamin asked.

"Oh, yes, and I'm also the Queen's granddaughter."

"Ah, that explains why you are always with her." Ristopher smiled. "It is a great honor to be standing next to you in battle." His words made Stella blush.

Their conversation was cut short when the Queen shouted over the group. "When the knights are ready, let us march!" Within a few minutes the entire formation was moving northeast, through the snow.

"Do you know how long it will take us to get there?" Radam asked Ristopher. "I have never walked to Chamoisee Canyon."

"By my guess, roughly three hours," Ristopher said after a brief thought. "We are a large group and therefore we are moving slowly."

"As long as we are not exhausted by the time we get there," Tenjamin muttered.

"Come now, son," Ristopher said. "We have trekked much more than that while hunting. We shall be fine."

Ristopher was right. After an hour of walking, Stella was not even tired. She was beginning to get excited; she longed to watch Stella the Subjugator fall. It was, however, cold, and Stella shook slightly from the blowing winds.

"Do not fret the cold," Tenjamin had noticed her shiver. "Once we reach the canyon, there will be no wind.

"Good, because all this shaking will make me a bad shot," Stella said, making Ristopher laugh.

As they reached the second hour of their journey, Stella noticed that the snow was not as deep and it was not as cold. By the third hour, they had reached the edge of the canyon and near the center of the southern cliff. Stella could now see Mullitor flying above, circling the battleground.

"Halt!" shouted Queen Iona, and the formation stopped. Stella nearly stepped into the person in front of her. She peered through the crowd and saw, a hundred yards ahead, a large group of minotaurs. There had to be at least two hundred of them, all dressed in red armor. They were carrying every weapon imaginable: swords, maces, pole arms and more. In the back of the group, she saw Stella Cinereous, dressed in pure white and her long blonde hair was in a braid. She was mounted on what looked like an overgrown flamingo, and she had two daggers sheathed around her waist.

"Double lines!" Queen Iona gave an order. The people moved until they were twenty people to a line. Stella shifted slightly to the right to allow room. "Jerot, when you are ready, you may draw the Battle Line!"

Jerot left the group and began walking towards the center of the battlefield. Stella saw the blonde woman also give an order, and one minotaur left his formation to walk to the center as well. He was larger than the others, and his red armor was trimmed in gold; he had to be the lead knight.

"What are they doing?" asked Radam.

"They are going to draw the Battle Line," said Tenjamin. "Our job is to make sure none of the enemy cross it."

Stella watched as Jerot and the minotaur met in the center of the field. After a few seconds of insulting each other, they both drew their swords and plunged them into the ground. Then Jerot dragged his sword along the ground southward, while the minotaur went northward. Once the minotaur reached the edge of the cliff, he pulled out his sword and sheathed it. Jerot did the same once his sword went from the red soil to the snow. They both then went back to their armies.

"At the ready!" commanded Queen Iona. Everyone in front of Stella pulled out their weapons, and the archers set arrows onto their bows, crouching down on one knee. Stella took an arrow out of her quiver and placed it against her bow, and she got down on one knee as well. She glanced at the minotaurs and saw they, too, were ready.

Mullitor was watching the action from above and, when he saw that everyone was ready, he let out a loud roar. The battle had begun.

"Charge!" shouted Jerot and, like a flash, the melee-wielding people flew forward. The minotaurs advanced and everyone collided on the Battle Line in a loud clash of weapons and shields. Stella kept her eye on the battle, waiting to strike should a minotaur break the line. Radam took shelter behind Stella.

After a few minutes, Stella got her chance. A large brown minotaur had broken the line. He was rushing straight towards Tenjamin. She took aim and fired, hitting him in the shoulder. Tenjamin and Ristopher also fired, their arrows making contact with the minotaur's chest. He fell only a few feet from Tenjamin, and lay still as stone.

"Good shot, Stella," said Ristopher.

"Not really," Stella grabbed another arrow. "I was aiming for his head."

The battle continued for several minutes. Swords and spears glinted in the setting sun and cries of determination and pain echoed around the canyon. Stella's eyes were glued on the battle. She was not going to aim poorly again.

Then, like a flare of blinding light, she saw Stella Cinereous. She was no longer on her mount, and wielded two long daggers made of gold. Anyone who approached her was instantly killed, splattering blood onto her white dress. She was clearly in Stella's sight and Stella couldn't resist. She pulled back her arrow and breathed deeply. This was it. This was the moment to end all the suffering the Cobalian people had endured. Stella was about to fire, when something else caught her eye.

It was Jerot. He had cut his way through the minotaurs and was now advancing on Stella the Subjugator himself. He had lost his helmet in the battle and his tabard was ripped and covered in blood. He was blocking Stella's shot.

"Dang it, Jerot," Stella lowered her bow. He was in the way. She aimed again at the two combatants, sword and daggers flying between them, blurred by their speed. Stella Cinereous was slowly pushing Jerot north along the Battle Line, then they were fighting at the edge of the cliff. *Please be careful*, Stella thought, trying desperately to get a clear shot.

The blonde woman crossed her daggers, blocking Jerot's sword. With a swift flick of her wrist, she sent Jerot's sword up into the air, then it landed on the ground several feet away. Stella watched in panic as, with one quick movement, Stella the Subjugator stabbed Jerot straight into his chest. His armor stopped the dagger no better than butter would stop a knife. The dagger went completely through his body. Before Stella could react, the blonde woman yanked the dagger out of Jerot and raised her foot, kicking him square in the chest. Jerot stumbled and then plummeted over the edge of the cliff.

"No!" Stella screamed and, without a second thought, raced towards the cliff.

"Stella, no!" Radam shouted, but all she could hear was the beating of her own heart. Everything moved in slow motion, as if her legs were made of lead. She ran barely two feet when a dark purple blur flew down the canyon after Jerot. *Please, Mullitor, catch him*, she thought. Stella managed to run a little farther when Mullitor emerged from the canyon and landed in the center of the Battle Line. People and minotaurs fled in fear at the sight of the dragon. He let out a deafening roar and, as Stella ran towards him, she could see he was holding Jerot like a baby.

It felt like an eternity, but Stella finally reached them. Tears streamed down her face as she looked at Jerot. His eyes were closed and she couldn't tell if he was breathing.

"Stella!" Radam had caught up to her. "What on earth are you doing? You are in danger."

"He still lives," Mullitor said. He too had tears trickling from his eyes. "But barely."

Like a flash, the Queen and Tuptup were at Stella's side. The Queen took one look at Jerot and shrieked, "Oh God, my baby!" Queen Iona fell upon his chest and cried.

Stella had a thought, "Quick! Take him to the cavern. The crystals, they will heal him."

"My friend, his wound is far too great," said Mullitor. "The crystals will not save him in time."

"Please!" Stella's voice was desperate. "Grandma, go with him." Mullitor looked into her eyes and knew he couldn't argue.

"Very well," he said, "but I make no promises." Tuptup helped the Queen onto Mullitor's back before he spread his wings and took off with Jerot towards the Cave of Eternal Blaze.

"Stella, we have got to go back," Radam clawed at her pant leg. "It is not safe out here."

"I'm afraid you are not going anywhere," said a voice behind Stella. She turned to see the blonde woman approaching. "So, it seems we are standing face to face on the battlefield," Stella the Subjugator's lips curled in pleasure. "Just the way I like it. Fight me to the death for your precious ring."

Stella stared at the blonde woman, a new hatred rising inside her. "You got it." She said.

"Stella, no!" Radam grew afraid. "Remember what Mistis said."

"Mistis can shove it," Stella snapped. She walked over to Jerot's sword, still in the ground. She pulled it out of the red soil and found it amazingly light for such a large sword. Blood was splattered on the hilt. She turned and began to walk towards Stella Cinereous. "Bring it, witch."

Stella the Subjugator laughed. "I'll make this easy for you. You will die by only one dagger." She threw a dagger to the ground and it landed in front of Radam, who immediately jumped on it to keep it put.

"Not a wise move," Stella held Jerot's sword in both hands, "because I'm going to kick your butt." She swung the sword at the blonde woman who blocked easily with her dagger. Stella continued to swing and thrust the sword at Stella Cinereous, but Stella the Subjugator blocked every attack.

"Defend, Stella," Tuptup shouted at her. "You're only going to get tired if you keep on offense."

"Yes," Stella Cinereous mocked Tuptup, "we wouldn't want you to die exhausted. It's my turn now." She jabbed at Stella with her dagger, but Stella was able to parry the dagger and keep it away from her. "Very good. You must have had a good teacher."

"The best" Stella panted. She was getting tired. Sweat poured from her brow.

"Not good enough, I'm afraid," Stella the Subjugator again thrust her dagger at Stella. This time, she caught Jerot's sword and twisted it out of Stella's hands. Stella immediately ran to retrieve it, but she felt the blonde woman grab her by her ponytail and fling her to the ground.

"Foul!" cried Radam. Stella rolled over to see Stella Cinereous staring down at her, an evil grin on her face.

"Enough!" Stella the Subjugator said. "It is time to die." She raised her dagger high above her head. Stella shielded her face with her arm. This was it; she knew she would never see her grandmother, Tuptup, Mullitor, or even Jerot ever again. She held her breath, waiting for the moment of death.

Stella heard a loud shriek. She moved her arm to see Stella Cinereous had dropped to her knees. From her chest, the dagger she had thrown aside was sticking out from the back. Behind her stood the young messenger servant of Mistis that had given Stella the message, the one who had served Stella and Mistis lunch in the Hall of Sight. His orange hair was wild, and his eyes burned with an intense anger.

"No fair!" screamed Stella the Subjugator, as she looked down at the tip of the dagger jutting from her chest.

Stella got up and ran to get Jerot's sword. "Maybe no one taught you, but life isn't fair," and with a final swing she cut off Stella Cinereous' head. The blonde woman's body fell forward, dead.

The Cobalian army cheered Stella's victory. She turned to the servant. "Thank you, whoever you are," she said.

"Don't you recognize who I am?" The young man spoke for the first time, but Stella had heard that voice before. It took her a second before she realized someone was missing from the battlefield.

"Radam?"

"Yes. I was told to protect you. I had no choice," Radam said.

"But how?" Stella was confused.

"I'm a shape shifter," Radam said. "I prefer my cat form, but I can take on any living form I wish."

"You should have told me sooner." Stella couldn't help but smile.

"I didn't think it was important." Radam said. "Uh-oh," he pointed behind Stella and she turned.

The minotaur that had drawn the Battle Line with Jerot was walking towards them, though he was clearly unarmed. Stella handed Radam Jerot's sword.

The minotaur stood a few feet from Stella and spoke. "You have killed Stella Cinereous."

"Yes, I have," Stella's voice was soft yet wary. The minotaur got down on one knee and lowered his head in respect. The rest of the minotaur army did the same. "You have freed us from her strict rule. We are in your debt. Give us an order and we will obey."

"Do you have a home?" Stella asked.

The minotaur looked up at her. "Yes, we come from an island far south of here. It is called Fallow."

"Then I order you to go home," Stella placed her hand on the minotaur's shoulder. "Live out your lives in peace and prosperity."

The minotaur smiled and tears filled his eyes. As he stood, he said, "Now that is an order we will gladly obey." He turned to his army and said a few words in a strange language. The army all stood, picked up their weapons and their dead, turned southward and started the long journey home.

The Confession

"We have to get back to the cave quickly," Stella turned to Tuptup with alarm. "I have to know if Jerot's okay."

"I'm afraid that's not an option," Tuptup shook his head. "You could take the Queen's horse and go on ahead but, even at her fastest, you would not make it there in under an hour."

"Maybe I can help," Radam said as he handed Jerot's sword back to Stella. "Stand back. This could get big." He crossed his arms over his chest and, in the blink of an eye, he shape-shifted into a dragon. He looked just like Mullitor, only his fleece-like hide was orange instead of the dark purple.

"Radam, you're a genius," Stella tucked Jerot's sword behind her belt and hopped onto Radam's back. "Will you be all right without me?"

"Don't you worry," Tuptup rocked on his feet and pulled Adraham's rolled-up parchment from his hip pouch. "I have controlled an army or two, in my time. Once we properly identify and bury all the dead, we will head back."

"Then I'll see you at the cavern," Stella turned to Radam. "Let's go!" Radam spread his wings and rose into the air. The ride was not as smooth as Mullitor's.

"You'll have to forgive me," Radam said. "I've never flown at this size before."

"Just as long as you're fast, it's okay," Stella gripped onto Radam's neck. Indeed he was fast. The trees below them were a blur and even the clouds above weren't moving as fast as Radam. In fact, he seemed faster than Mullitor. In a matter of minutes, they had reached the cave. Stella dismounted as she grabbed a lantern, and Radam shifted back into a cat. They walked into the tunnel and Stella immediately searched for Jerot.

He was not hard to find, for Stella spotted Mullitor and knew Jerot would be nearby. The dragon was behind the Queen's tent. Jerot was lying on a cot surrounded by a group of crystals. His armor had been removed and a large bandage was wrapped around his entire chest; a fist size bloodstain had formed on the bandage and he was unconscious. The crystals glowed and pulsated as three Healers busied themselves around the wounded knight, reading healing recipes, mixing elixirs and chanting. One of the Healers was Behitha, whom Stella approached.

"How is he?"

Behitha frown slightly. "I'm afraid we've done all we can do. The dagger went completely through a lung and just barely missed his heart. All that can save him now are the crystals, and his will to live."

"Are you sure?" Radam asked. "There isn't anything else you can do?"

"We are still looking in the books, but we have very limited resources."

"Thank you," was all Stella could say. She and Radam walked over and sat next to her grandmother. The Queen was holding Jerot's hand, her face streaked with tears. "Grandma," Stella said, "I defeated Stella Cinereous."

"That's wonderful, dear," Queen Iona didn't take her eyes off of Jerot. She took a deep breath before she spoke again. "I have said my peace to Jerot. I will leave you alone so you can have your turn."

"You act like he's already dead," Stella said. The Queen looked at her with sadness in her eyes.

"Stella, we have exhausted all hope. If there is anything you want to say, do it now, before it's too late." She stood up, picked up Radam and went back into her tent. Mullitor gently nudged Stella with his snout before retreating to another part of the cavern. The Healers also left, defeated in their vain attempt to save Jerot.

Stella took Jerot's hand and gave it a slight squeeze, but he didn't respond. His hand was cold as stone.

"Did you hear?" Stella watched his shallow breathing. "I defeated Stella Cinereous," Stella took Jerot's sword out from behind her belt and laid it on the cavern floor next to Jerot. "I brought your sword back for you," A soft gurgling could be heard coming from Jerot's chest. No doubt it was blood filling into his lung. Stella couldn't hold back any longer and she broke down in tears.

"Oh Jerot," she could barely get the words out, "please don't die. You can't die." She lowered her head so that her lips were close to his ear. Even though she was alone with him, she wanted only Jerot to hear her next words. "Jerot, you were right. I do have feelings for you. I love you."

Stella laid her head on his shoulder and softly hummed her favorite lullaby, the Dvorak Symphony #9, 2nd movement filled the air around them. She quietly sung the words, which had new meaning for her.

> *Night my love, sleep my love,*
> *Dreams will entertain.*
> *Goodbye my love, precious love,*
> *Till we meet again.*
> *Perfect worlds and happy times,*
> *There is no more pain.*
> *Flowering fields and bright sunsets,*
> *To ease all of your strain.*
> *Night my love, rest my love,*
> *Close your eyes tonight.*
> *Goodbye my love, beloved love,*
> *Enjoy fantasy's delight.*

"You sing beautifully," a weak voice whispered in Stella's ear. She sat up to see Jerot had awakened. His eyes were not the usual vivid blue, but dull gray. Stella began to cry tears of joy.

"Jerot, you're awake," Stella choked on her words. "You heard me."

"Every word," Jerot squeezed Stella's hand. "I love you too. More than you can imagine."

Stella bent down, placed her hands on Jerot's cheeks and kissed him, over and over again. She tried carefully not to hurt him. Her tears fell upon his face. With all his strength, Jerot wrapped his arms around Stella. She looked in his eyes again: still dull, but she saw a glimmer of blue.

"Should I call the Healers?" Stella wiped her tears from Jerot's face.

"Not yet," Jerot began to cry his own tears of joy, "You are all I need right now to heal me."

***

Stella opened her eyes to find herself in the Welcome Garden. She would have loved to stay and smell the wonderful fragrances, but Dekel was already there with Jerot's Friesian. It had been two weeks since the battle, and all was almost normal.

"Good morning, ma'am," Dekel smiled and placed a cloak around

Stella. "We are having a January thaw, so you shouldn't be so cold today."

"That's good," Stella mounted the horse while Dekel took the reins. "The cold is starting to wear thin on me."

Dekel led the Friesian into the forest and indeed it was warmer than usual. The snow was thin enough that patches of the ground could be seen and little forest critters ran to and fro in delight of the weather. The sky was cloudless and the sun cast long shadows of early morning. It was a beautiful day, but now every day was beautiful to Stella.

Once inside Cobalian, Stella got off the horse, but did not head to the castle. No, she was going somewhere more important. Stella had only been to the castle a few times since she had defeated Stella the Subjugator. She followed a path south of the trade quarter and around to the back of the castle. People greeted Stella and waved; she was their heroine and was well-honored in the city. Around the castle, she found a large stone building, which had a sign of a leaf hanging on the front. This was the Healers' Medical Building, where Jerot had been for two weeks. He was still wounded, but every day he was getting better.

Stella entered the building and was greeted by some of the Healers. She took a left and then a right before entering a room where she saw Jerot. He was sitting in a large bed, his hair wet from a recent bath, and a Healer placing a new bandage around his chest. Stella got a small glimpse of his wound; it was not as bad as it was. Jerot smiled when he saw her, his eyes were still clouded in gray, but they brightened at the sight of Stella.

"You are just in time for breakfast," he said as Stella walked over to the chair by his bed, sat down and took his hand.

"How are you feeling today?" Stella had asked this same question for two weeks.

"It's hurts a little when I breathe, but other than that, it's okay."

"More than okay," said the Healer, a bald elderly man. "The wound on your back is completely healed. Now, if we can just get the one on the front to close, we'll be in good shape."

"That's great news since it was starting to gather pus a few days ago," Stella said.

"Indeed," the Healer gently helped Jerot relax on his mound of pillows. "Now, let me go get your meal," and he left the room.

When Stella could no longer hear the Healer's footsteps, she leaned in and kissed Jerot. "I missed you."

"I did too," Jerot said before kissing Stella again. If it wasn't for the Healer's return, they could have kissed each other all day. The Healer returned, holding a large tray of food.

"Soup's on!" said the Healer cheerfully. "Well, it's more like French toast, but you get the idea." He set the tray down in Jerot's lap before excusing himself again. Stella held the fork and fed Jerot, giggling when she dripped syrup on his chin.

"Let me get that for you," Stella took a napkin and wiped the syrup away. She took a bite of the toast. "Quite good."

"Not as good as Tuptup's, but I'll still eat it." Jerot took a sip of orange juice.

"Did I hear my name?" Tuptup entered the room, startling Stella.

"My goodness," Stella put a hand to her chest. "Don't do that again."

"Sorry," Tuptup blushed. The Queen entered behind him. For the first time since Stella has known her as Queen, she had started to show her age. Her wrinkles seemed deeper and her blue eyes were reddened from crying. She rushed to Jerot's side.

"I heard from the Healers that one wound is healed," Queen Iona tried to smile. "I hope this means you are feeling better."

"As long as I have a good nurse, I'm fine," Jerot took Stella's hand. She gently patted his hand before pulling away. They had made a pact to not tell anyone they loved each other.   At least, not yet. Stella slightly blushed from Jerot's affection.

"I'm sure she is spectacular," Queen Iona said, "but today is Friday. Isn't that the day you visit Mullitor?" she asked Stella.

"It is. We are going to visit Radam and Mistis for lunch," Stella gave Jerot his fork so he could finish eating.

"Well, that sounds like a wonderful adventure," said Queen Iona. "Tell Mistis I said hello."

"Don't worry," Stella winked. "I'm sure she already knows." Stella's old joke still made everyone laugh. Once Jerot was finished eating, the Queen and Tuptup informed him that the townspeople were adjusting nicely to being back in Cobalian. The Queen had checked on everyone, every day, to ensure all was well.

"All the knights miss you," said Tuptup, "but they won't admit it."

"Ah, you got to love those guys." Jerot closed his eyes. "I hope you don't mind, but I think I'm tired. A nap sounds good about now."

"Yes, a nap will help you heal," Queen Iona brushed a piece of Jerot's hair from his face. "I should go and check on the rest of the city," she turned to Stella. "Would you like to come?"

"No, I'll stay here," Stella removed the tray from Jerot's lap and placed it on a table by the door. "I told Mullitor to meet me here."

"Well, all right," Queen Iona walked over to Stella and kissed her on the cheek. "See you at dinnertime." She and Tuptup left the room.

Stella sat down by Jerot and took his hand. "Is there anything I can do to make you more comfortable?"

"Yes," Jerot slouched down into his bed, trying to relax. "Sing to me."

"Oh, I don't think that's a good idea. I'm not that good."

"You don't give yourself credit. Your singing healed me," Jerot squeezed her hand. Stella looked at the door to make sure no one was coming, and then started to sing *Hotel California*. She sang it softly, so only Jerot could hear it. By the time she reached the second verse, he was fast asleep. Stella stopped singing and leaned in to tenderly kiss Jerot on the forehead.

"Sleep well, brave knight," she said before heading out of the building to wait for Mullitor.

www.ingramcontent.com/pod-product-compliance
Lightning Source LLC
Chambersburg PA
CBHW072317020726
47501CB00002B/542